LOVE'S HELPER

LOVE'S MAGIC SERIES BOOK 17

BETTY MCLAIN

This book is dedicated to everyone unafraid to accept help from their guardian angel.

CAST OF CHARACTERS

Minnie Kelp – Works in daycare – wants to be teacher

Bobby Kelp – Minnie's brother – newspaper reporter

Margo Croan – Minnie and Bobby's mother

Arnie Croan – Minnie and Bobby's stepfather

Sandor (Sandy) Mase – Bobby's childhood friend -works for Avorn Security

Salvadori (Sal) Mase _ Sandy's brother – Bobby's friend – works for Avorn Security

Mr. and Mrs. Mase – Next door neighbors of the Croan family

Louanne – Minnie's friend

Alex Avorn – Owner and operator of Avorn Security

Miriam Avorn – Alex's wife

Michael (Micky) Ansel – Avorn Security agent

Andrew Salto – Avorn Security agent

Dr. Parks – Avorn Security doctor on call

Lila – Dr. Parks' nurse

Stan Varin – Avorn Security agent

FBI Agents – Slocome and Hatch

Trey and Lori Loden III – husband and wife team working for
Avorn Securities

Lynn - Desk clerk third floor

Brenda – Alex's personal assistant

Sally Swills – works in beauty parlor in Avorn building -Has custody
of her

Nephew, Andy's son – Amory Hanks

Andy Hanks – Armed intruder in Avorn building looking for his son

Jessie Dills – Andy Hanks' friend – wanted to help his friend

Judge Barbara Leeks – Judge in Hanks custody case

PROLOGUE

MINNIE WAS BENDING over as she made her way into the under-ground tunnel leading between her house to the storm cellar next door. Her guardian angel warned her she was in danger. Her stepfa-ther and two of his friends were in the living room drinking and talking loudly. Minnie heard them say her name several times. She had been afraid to go out the front door by them, but she knew of another way out, so she grabbed her backpack and stuffed a couple of changes of clothes, her phone, and purse in it. Minnie put on her coat and picked up a flashlight. She went into the closet and pushed the button on the side of the wooden box holding extra blankets. The box slid out to show the opening below.

Minnie climbed down the stairs and lay her backpack down. She then climbed back up and pushed the button to move the box back in place. and turned the lock to keep the box from being opened from above.

While she was standing there on the stairs, she heard someone enter her room. She stood very still, not daring to move.

"Hey, Arnie, I thought you said the girl was in her room," shouted one of her stepfather's friends.

Minnie heard more footsteps.

"She must have gone somewhere when I was in the bathroom," said Arnie. "No matter, we'll catch her when she comes back."

"Yeah, okay," said his friend.

Minnie heard footsteps go out. They must have left the door open. Minnie did not hear it close. She sat quietly in the dark tunnel, holding her breath in case one of them came back.

The tunnel had been dug ten years before by her brother and his friends, Sandy and Sal Mase. The boys had dug the tunnel and built the storm shelters during the summer while they were out of school. Bobby had made her promise not to tell anyone about the tunnel. Minnie had known about the tunnel from the time it was built. The boys had let her help by watching out for anyone coming while they were working underground. She was nine at the time and would do anything for her big brother and his friends. Minnie and Bobby's mother had been at work. She worked at the school as a janitor. Summer school was in session, so she didn't get off for the summer. She was glad for the paycheck.

The Mase boys' mother was at home, but she only knew about the storm shelter in their back yard. She did not know about the tunnel or about the storm shelter room the boys had built underneath Bobby's room. The boys had built a secret door in Bobby's closet. It had stairs leading down into the room and the tunnel.

The Mase boys had worked part time with their father in his construction business. He had given them left over material to build the storm shelter with. He had not known they were building one for Bobby, too. The tunnel was hidden from view. The boys had built a hidden door in the side of the Mase storm shelter so their mother or father would not see the tunnel when they came to see their storm shelter.

Minnie was hoping the tunnel was still in good shape. It had not been used in a long time. When Bobby had moved out and got his own place, after going to work at the newspaper, the room had become Minnie's.

Minnie eased down the stairs, quietly, making sure not to make any noise. She picked up her backpack and, turning on the flashlight, she bent over and started down the small tunnel toward the storm shelter in the Mase's back yard.

ONE

THESE THINGS WERE RUNNING through Minnie's mind as she made her way through the tunnel. She was glad for a strong flashlight. It would have been scary going through the tunnel without it.

Minnie eased her way into the Mase storm shelter. The boys had some beanbag chairs inside. They had used the shelter as a clubhouse. Minnie eased over to the door and cracked it open to look around. She could see one of her stepfather's friends sitting on the front porch of her home. He was drinking a beer.

Minnie eased back and sat on one of the chairs. She put her backpack down and took out her phone. Minnie knew it would not do any good to call her brother. She had been calling him for a week without getting an answer. He was not calling her back. Minnie sighed. She knew something was wrong. Bobby would never ignore her this way.

Minnie scrolled through her list of contacts. She had both Sandy and Sal's numbers listed. Minnie punched in Sandy's number and hit send. The phone rang only twice before Sandy answered.

"Hello," said Sandy.

"Hello, Sandy," said Minnie softly.

"Yes, who is this?" asked Sandy.

"It's Minnie, I need help," said Minnie.

Sandy sat up abruptly. "What's wrong, Minnie? Are you hurt?"

"No, I got away from them before they could hurt me," said Minnie.

"Got away from who?" demanded Sandy.

"Arnie and his friends, they were drinking and talking about teaching me how to be a woman. My guardian angel told me to hide, so I did," said Minnie.

Sandy cursed, and wished he could get his hands on Arnie. Minnie did not deserve to have to deal with the jerk or his friends.

"Where are you, Minnie?" he asked.

"I came through the tunnel. I'm in your storm shelter. I can't leave. One of Arnie's friends is sitting on our porch drinking. I think they have done something to Bobby. He has been gone for almost a week and he is not answering his phone or calling me back. I heard them mention his name several times, but I could not hear what they were saying," said Minnie.

"You stay where you are. Don't try to come out. I'll be there as soon as I can," said Sandy.

"Okay, thanks," said Minnie. She hung up and leaned back in the chair to wait on Sandy.

Sandy hung up his phone and went into the kitchen of the apartment he shared with his brother Sal. Sal was eating a sandwich. He looked up when Sandy entered. When he saw Sandy's face, he looked at him alertly.

"What's wrong?" asked Sal.

"I just got a call from Minnie. She went through the tunnel and is hiding in our storm shelter. She was getting away from Arnie and his goon friends. She said Bobby has been missing for a week," said Sandy.

Sal dropped his sandwich and rose. "Let's go," he said.

Sandy turned and led the way out to his car. They both quickly entered the car and Sandy headed for their childhood home.

When they reached the house, Sandy pulled the car into the garage.

"You go in and tell Mom we are getting something from the storm shelter. I'll get Minnie and hide her in the car," said Sandy.

"Okay," said Sal. He turned and headed inside.

Sandy eased open the back door in the garage, he looked over next door. The porch was empty. They had seen the man sitting out there when they drove up. He must have gone inside. Sandy walked over and opened the door of the storm shelter.

Minnie looked at him with big, scared looking, brown eyes. When she saw who was there, she jumped up and threw her arms around him and squeezed tightly.

"It's alright," said Sandy hugging her back. "You're safe. I won't let anything happen to you," he promised.

Minnie pulled back slightly. She had tears in her eyes. "I was so scared," she whispered.

Sandy picked up her backpack and flashlight. He kept one arm around her to guide her toward the door. "We are going through the back door of the garage and you are going to duck down in the back seat. We don't want Arnie and his friends to know where you have gone," said Sandy.

Sandy held her close to his side and made sure he was between her and the house next door. He had left the door open, so they entered with no trouble. Sandy opened the back door of his car and had her lie down on the seat. He put her backpack and flashlight inside; and leaned down to speak to her.

"I have to run inside to get Sal and say a quick hello to Mom. I'll be right back," he said. Sandy closed the door quietly and then, after making sure the back, garage door was closed, he hurried inside.

"Hi, Mom," said Sandy giving her a quick hug. "You ready to go?" he asked Sal.

"Yeah," said Sal. "Just as soon as I get this piece of chocolate cake Mom is cutting for me."

Their Mom shook her head; but grinned at her boys. She was

glad they liked her cooking so much. "Do you boys have to be in such a hurry?" she asked.

"We are on a case. We just stopped to pick up something," said Sandy.

"I didn't know you had anything important in the storm shelter," remarked Mrs. Mase.

"It was just some drawings we thought might come in handy," said Sal.

"Well, here is some cake for both of you. Next time come when you can stay longer," she replied handing Sal a bowl with several pieces of cake in it.

Sal took the bowl and kissed her cheek. "Thanks, Mom." he said.

"Yeah, thanks, Mom," said Sandy giving her a kiss on the cheek as they left.

They got into the car and Sandy glanced into the back seat and smiled at Minnie. Minnie smiled back at him.

Sal looked back over the seat and smiled at Minnie and said, "Hi." Minnie smiled back at him and said, "Hi."

Both guys faced forward as they drove away from the house. Sandy noticed the man sitting on the porch next door. He was opening a new can of beer.

Sal and Sandy exchanged a look; but didn't say anything.

Sandy drove to their apartment and drove inside the garage. They did not want anyone seeing Minnie. They did not know what was going on; and were not taking any chances with Minnie's life.

Sandy got out and opened the back, car door and helped Minnie out. He picked up her backpack and flashlight and guided her inside. Sal had gone ahead and unlocked the door. Sal left the cake on the kitchen counter and led the way into the living room.

Minnie dropped into a chair and Sandy dropped her backpack and flashlight on the floor beside the chair. Sandy sat in the chair next to her and Sal sat on the sofa.

"Can you tell us what happened?" asked Sandy.

Minnie looked up at him. Her eyes teared up. "Thank you for

coming to get me," she said. "I didn't know who else to call, after Bobby has dropped out of sight."

"You can always call us when you need help. We are here for you. How long has it been since you heard from Bobby?" asked Sandy.

"It's been a week. He came by the house and left some papers with me. He told me not to tell anyone about them and then he left. I have tried to call him several times a day since, but he doesn't answer and he doesn't call me back," said Minnie.

"Do you have the papers?" asked Sal.

"Yes, they are here in my backpack," said Minnie. She opened her backpack and drew out a hand full of papers from between her clothes and handed them to Sandy.

Sandy took the papers and started looking at them. He cursed and handed the papers to Sal as he finished reading them.

Sal cursed also as he read the papers.

"What's wrong?" asked Minnie.

"Did you read these papers?" asked Sandy.

Minnie shook her head. "No, Bobby told me not to. He said to keep them safe for him," said Minnie.

"These papers are records of Arnie and his buddies taking bribes to let drugs be delivered in our town. It also mentions a child trafficking payoff. It looks like Bobby had an informant, and he was planning to write a story about this and expose Arnie and his friends," said Sal.

Minnie gasped. "I knew they were up to no good. Do you think they found out and they took Bobby?"

"Probably, they may have been trying to get him to tell where these papers are. They know if anyone finds out about this they will go to jail, but since they are all working for the police, they are in position to stop anyone finding out," said Sandy.

"We need to get some help and find out where they are holding Bobby," said Sal.

"You need to call your mom before she goes home and tell her you went to the movies with a girlfriend and are going to spend the night with her," said Sandy looking at Minnie.

Minnie looked at him for a minute. "Do you think he will hurt Mom?" she asked.

"I don't think so. She's his cover. Arnie will take care to keep her in the dark. He will probably send his friends packing before your mom gets home," said Sandy.

Minnie nodded. She accepted his words. Minnie knew he worked for a security company and he would know much more about such things. Minnie got out her phone and called her friend Louanne.

"Hi, Louanne, this is Minnie. I was wondering if you could cover for me if my mom calls you. I'm going to tell her I am spending the night with you," asked Minnie.

"Sure, if she calls, I'll tell her you are in the shower. What are you up to?" asked Louanne.

"I'll tell you all about it later. I have to call Mom now. Oh, if she says anything, we had a great time shopping and at the movie this afternoon," said Minnie.

Minnie hung up the phone to Louanne's laughter. She punched in her mom's number.

"Hi, Mom, I just wanted to let you know, since I have a few days off, I called Louanne and we decided to get together to go shopping and then to see a movie this afternoon, and I am going to be spending the night with her," said Minnie.

"Okay, Minnie, you two girls have a good time," said Margo Croan. "I'll see you tomorrow."

"Thanks, Mom, we will," said Minnie.

Minnie hung up the phone and looked at Sandy. "I hate lying to Mom. I wish she had never fallen for Arnie. We were doing fine until he entered the picture. The last five years have been very hard trying to stay under Arnie's radar," said Minnie.

"Has he threatened you before?" asked Sandy his hand curling into a fist.

"No, but the way he looked at me made my skin crawl. My guardian angel has protected me and helped me to avoid him," said Minnie.

Sandy relaxed slightly. Minnie was very important to him. He had tried not to let his feelings for her show because she was Bobby's little sister, but he had always felt like he should look out for her. If Arnie tried to hurt her, he would make sure he didn't get a chance to hurt anyone else.

"We need to round up some of the guys and follow Arnie's friends and see if they will lead us to Bobby," said Sal.

"Yeah," agreed Sandy. "You call Alex and see who is available. Fill him in on what's going on and I'll get Minnie some food and settle her in my room. I'll bunk with you," said Sandy.

"I don't want to put you out of your room," protested Minnie. "I can sleep on the sofa."

"It's better if you stay in my room," said Sandy. "If anyone comes in, they won't see you, and if we have to go out, you can just stay in there and don't answer the door."

"Okay," agreed Minnie. "I'm sorry I'm causing you so much trouble."

"It's no trouble. You can always come to us when you need us. We will always be here for you. You and Bobby are family," said Sandy.

Minnie frowned, but she continued to follow Sandy into the kitchen.

Sandy pulled out some sandwich makings and sat them on the counter. He pulled a soda out of the fridge and sat it in front of Minnie. Minnie popped the can open and took a long drink. She had been afraid to go past Arnie and his friends to get either food or drinks. She was glad Sandy was making her a sandwich.

"I can make the sandwich," said Minnie.

"It's almost ready," said Sandy with a smile. "Just enjoy it."

"Thanks," said Minnie taking a big bite and savoring the taste.

Sandy opened the bowl with the cake in it and, seeing four slices in the bowl, he put a slice on a plate and sat it in front of Minnie.

"Ummmm, it smells great," said Minnie.

"Mom made it," said Sandy.

"I love your mom's cake," said Minnie taking a bite after finishing her sandwich.

"Would you like another sandwich?" asked Sandy.

"No, this is fine," said Minnie eating more cake.

Sal came into the room. "Alex is sending Andrew and Micky to help us. They will be here soon." He grabbed a fork and plate and put a piece of the cake on his plate. Sal took a large bite an expression of bliss on his face as he savored the cake.

Minnie laughed at the expression on his face.

"I'm not taking any chances with my Mom's cake," said Sal smiling as he took another bite.

Sandy shook his head. "I put your half, eaten sandwich in the refrigerator." He told Sal.

"Thanks," said Sal as he concentrated on his cake.

Sandy turned to Minnie. "If you are finished, I'll show you your room before the guys get here," he told Minnie.

"I'm ready," said Minnie rising and following Sandy.

"There are towels in the bathroom and extra blankets in the hall closet. I don't know how long we will be, but don't answer the door if anyone knocks. If you get hungry or thirsty, help yourself to whatever you want in the refrigerator. We will get back as soon as we can," said Sandy.

He reached over and pulled her into his arms for a hug. "I am glad you are alright," said Sandy.

Minnie hugged him back. "Thanks," she whispered. She reluctantly pulled away. She loved being so close to Sandy, but she knew he didn't feel the same way she felt, and she did not want to take advantage of him.

Sandy gazed into her face for a minute. He really loved the thought of Minnie being in his room so close he could feel her presence. He had been dreaming about having her here for a long time. He just wished it was under different circumstances.

There was a knock at the door, and he smiled at her and turned away giving her hand a final squeeze. He closed the door as he left and went to open door.

TWO

SANDY SMILED and greeted Andrew and Micky as Sal let them into the apartment.

"Thanks for coming to help," said Sandy.

"Alex said Bobby Kelp was missing," said Micky.

"Yes, we think he was onto a story. He had an informant in a policeman corruption case and the main suspect is his stepfather. We think his stepfather found out and is holding him somewhere. We are hoping to follow Arnie or his friends and find out where they are holding Bobby," said Sandy.

"How did you find out about Bobby? Did he call you?" asked Andrew.

"No, Minnie called us," said Sandy. "She overheard Arnie and his friends talking about Bobby while they were sitting around drinking. When they started talking about raping her, she slipped out and hid at our place next door and called me."

Andrew and Micky both cursed. "Is she alright?" asked Andrew.

"Yes, she will be okay. Her guardian angel warned her in time," said Sandy. "We have her here and we are going to make sure Arnie and his friends stay far away from her."

"Let's go find Bobby," said Micky standing up and starting toward the door.

The others followed him out.

"I'll go with Micky while you go with Andrew," said Sal.

Sandy nodded his agreement. He led the way to his car while Sal and Micky loaded into Micky's car and started toward their childhood home. When they arrived in the neighborhood, they drove on by and turned around and parked down the street so they could view the Croan house and see when Arnie or his friends left.

Sandy parked down the street in the other direction so they would be prepared for the men leaving in either direction.

"They should be clearing out. It's almost five and I'm sure Arnie will want them gone before his wife gets home from work," said Sandy.

Just as he finished speaking the front door opened and the guys piled out. You could tell they had been drinking, but two of them piled into a car and backed out of the drive to leave. Arnie and the other guy stood talking for a minute before Arnie went back inside and the last man left. Sal and Micky had followed the first two, so Sandy and Andrew followed the last one. They stayed back, so he wouldn't see them, but he wasn't paying any attention to them he headed straight toward the warehouse district.

The man drove on past the warehouses to the end of the street. He stopped in front of an abandoned factory at the edge of town. He left his car parked in front and entered the door.

Sandy parked his car down the street and he and Andrew got out and walked around toward the back of the building. They heard a car coming and quickly hid behind some bushes.

The car stopped and parked beside the other car in front of the abandoned factory. Arnie's other two friends got out carrying two six packs of beer each. They entered the front door and went inside as the first man had done.

Sal and Micky soon joined Sandy and Andrew behind the bushes.

"They stopped at the store and picked up some beer before coming straight here," said Micky.

"We need to see inside so we can be sure Bobby is here," said Sal.

"Andrew and I were going to check behind the building and see if there was any way to get a look inside," said Sandy.

"Micky and I will check out the other side of the building. We can meet back here and decide what to do next," said Sal.

The guys split up and headed out to look around. Sandy and Andrew were disappointed to find the only windows in the back were three stories up and there was a chain lock on the rear door. They turned and went back to their hiding place to see if the other two had found anything.

Sal and Micky were waiting for them.

They are sitting around a table drinking," said Sal. "They have Bobby tied to a chair. He looks like he is unconscious. He is pretty beat up."

"Did you see any other way to get in the building?" asked Andrew.

Sal shook his head. "All I saw was the front door." said Sal.

"Maybe they will get drunk and pass out," offered Micky.

"We need to call Alex and let him know what is going on. I e-mailed him copies of Bobby's papers. Maybe he has some suggestions," said Sal.

The others nodded agreement and Sal took out his phone and turned it on to call Alex Avorn, their boss.

"I would like to be sure Bobby doesn't get caught in the crossfire before calling in the sheriff," said Alex.

Yeah," agreed Sal. "Do you think Trey could help if we over-power them?" asked Sal.

"I'm afraid we have to handle this without Trey. He called a short time ago. He's headed to the hospital with Lori, the baby is coming. Mariam is on her way over to the hospital, too. I was just waiting to hear from you before going myself," said Alex.

"Lori's having the baby," Sal said in an aside to the others.

There were some smiles from the other three. Lori and Trey were part of their family. They all worked for Avorn Security and were close. They had all been anxiously awaiting the arrival of Trey and Lori's daughter.

"Give them our best wishes when you get a chance," said Sal.

"I will. You guys keep an eye on the situation and use your best judgment. If you get a chance, tie them up, and after the baby comes, Trey can take care of them. If he can't, we will have to turn them and the evidence over to my contact in the FBI and let them take care of the situation," said Alex.

"Okay, Boss," said Sal hanging up the phone and looking at Sandy and the others.

"He said to keep watch and use our best judgment," said Sal.

They heard a noise from the front of the building and all of the guys made sure they could not be seen. The saw one of the men exit the building. He was leading another one by his arm. He opened his car door and pushed the man inside and slammed the door. He went around and entered the driver's side.

After he was passed the guys came out of hiding. "Didn't he come by himself?" asked Andrew.

"Yeah," agreed Sandy. "We need to see what we can do while there is only one person watching Bobby."

The four of them hurried around the building to see if they could see in the side window. Sandy tried the front door as they went by it. He then followed the others around the building. "The front door is not locked," he said.

They watched the remaining man get up and go into another room. "It looks like he has gone to the bathroom," said Sal. "Maybe we can slip in before he returns."

They quickly hurried to the front and slipped into the building. They heard a toilet flush and Sal and Micky hurried over to catch the man when he came into the room. Sandy and Andrew went to check on Bobby.

Sandy checked Bobby's pulse and gave a relieved sigh when he felt its beat. He held him while Andrew slipped behind him and cut the ropes binding Bobby to the chair. Sandy picked Bobby up in his arms and he and Andrew started for the front door.

The man opened the bathroom door and cursed when he saw the two of them on their way out with Bobby. He didn't have time to do anything before Sal had him unconscious on the floor. Sal and Micky dragged him over and tied him in the chair where Bobby had been tied. They even used the same ropes. They left him there and hurried after Sandy and Andrew.

Sandy was hurrying to his car. They had no idea how long the others would be gone and they wanted to get Bobby away so they could get him medical help.

Sandy put Bobby in the back seat of his car and he and Andrew quickly entered the front and headed for Avorn Security. Sal and Micky followed behind them.

They pulled into the underground garage and took the elevator to the third floor. When the elevator stopped on the third floor and they came out with Sandy carrying Bobby, Lynn, in charge of the third floor desk, rose to her feet with a gasp.

"What's happened?" she asked.

"He's been tortured. We need a key to one of the apartments on the sixth floor and you need to call the doctor. Tell him to bring a portable x-ray with him," said Sandy.

Lynn handed a key to Sal and picked up her phone. Sandy stopped suddenly and looked back at Lynn. "Do not let anyone know Bobby is here," said Sandy.

Lynn just nodded her head and waved them on as she talked to the doctor. The guys piled into another elevator to get to the sixth floor where Alex had four apartments to be used in emergency situations.

Sal opened the door to 602 and Sandy carried Bobby inside followed by the other three. Sandy carried him into one of the two bedrooms and placed him on the bed. Sandy removed bobby's shoes and socks. He did not want to do anything else until the doctor looked him over.

"What do you think we should do about the guy we left tied up?" asked Andrew.

"We will see what Alex wants to do," said Sal. "He said to use our own judgment. It was more important to get Bobby out of there before they could beat on him any more. He might not have made it if we had waited."

Andrew and Micky nodded their agreement. Sandy was concentrating on Bobby and didn't answer. He was thinking about Minnie and how upset she was going to be when she saw what had been done to her brother. He had to figure out a way to keep her safe and away from Arnie and his friends. He knew she was going to be worried about her mom, too.

Sandy sighed. Sal looked at him. "What's wrong?" he asked.

"I was thinking about Minnie and how we can keep her away from Arnie and his friends," said Sandy.

"Yeah," agreed Sal. "There is no way she can go back home. It's not safe." Sandy nodded and Andrew and Micky agreed with them.

"It's too bad she doesn't have a boyfriend. She could marry him and have the perfect reason to move out without arousing suspicioun," said Andrew.

Sandy looked at him startled. The idea of Minnie marrying someone else did not sit right with him.

"We'll figure something out," he remarked.

"Has Bobby showed any sign of waking up," asked Sal.

"No," said Sandy. "It may be better if he doesn't wake up until the doctor checks him over."

The others nodded agreement. There was a knock at the door and Sal went to open the door for the doctor. Micky went with him for back-up.

Sal opened the door and sighed in relief at seeing the doctor.

"Hello Sal," said Dr. Parks. "I understand someone needs my help."

"Yeah, a friend of ours was kidnapped and tortured. He's in the bedroom," said Sal leading the way into the bedroom.

"Why didn't you take him to the hospital?" asked Dr. Parks.

"Because his kidnappers were policeman, if we had carried him to the hospital, they would have made sure he didn't leave there alive," said Sandy hearing the question as the doctor entered the room.

Dr. Parks hurried over to the bed. When he saw what shape, Bobby was in he cursed. He listened to Bobby's heartbeat and then started looking him over for injuries. The doctor finished his exam and looked up at the guys. They were all waiting anxiously for his verdict.

"As far as I can tell," said Dr. Parks. "The worst of his injuries are on his right hand. His fingers have been broken. The rest of his body is very badly, bruised, and he is badly dehydrated and doesn't look like he has eaten in days. I will set his fingers and we can get these filthy rags off him and get him cleaned up before putting salve on the worst of his bruises."

Sandy and Sal started removing Bobby's torn and ragged clothing while Dr. Parks prepared to set the fingers on his right hand.

Dr. Parks set up a portable IV to start getting some fluids into Bobby.

"Is he going to be alright?" asked Micky.

"He should be fine," said Dr. Parks. "It will be a couple of months before he will be able to use this hand. He will have to go to therapy before he will have full flexibility." Dr. Parks looked up at the guys.

"How are you going to stop the police from coming after him again?" he asked.

"Alex is going to get his contact in the FBI on the case when he gets back from the hospital," said Sal. Dr. Parks looked up, startled.

Sal laughed softly. "Lori is in labor," he said.

Dr. Parks smiled and nodded and turned back to working on Bobby.

They threw Bobby's clothes into the trash and Sal brought a

washcloth, soap, and a pan of warm water. Sandy used the wet soapy cloth and began to clean the dirt and dried blood off Bobby while Dr. Parks worked on his fingers.

Sal emptied the water and brought fresh, clean water several times. When Dr. Parks finished setting and strapping Bobby's fingers, Sandy had Micky hold Bobby's head over the pan of water while he washed and dried his hair. When they were finished cleaning Bobby, they moved him over and changed the bed sheets and pillowcase. They then covered him with a sheet and left him to rest while they went into the living room to talk to Dr. Parks.

"Thanks for coming to help," said Sandy.

Dr. Parks nodded. "He's going to be okay. He should wake up tomorrow. Don't worry if he takes longer, he needs the rest to help with healing. I will leave several IV bags and I will send a nurse over to check on him later today. Will it be alright for her to stay the night to keep an eye on him?"

"Sure, one of us will stay with him and I will try to bring his sister to see him," said Sandy. "Make sure your nurse knows to not let anyone know Bobby is here."

"I will, but she knows not to discuss anything that happens at Avorn Security," said Dr. Parks.

The guys grinned at this observation. It was good to know Alex was watching out for them all.

Dr. Parks took one last look at Bobby before gathering his things and leaving. When he was gone, Sal looked at Sandy. "Are you going to bring Minnie here?" he asked.

"Yes, I'll make sure she isn't seen. She's worried about Bobby. She won't settle until she sees he's okay," said Sandy.

"We need to call Alex and update him on what's happening," said Micky.

Sal took out his phone and called Alex. When he hung up from talking to Alex, Sal looked at the others. They had been listening and were waiting to hear what Alex said.

"The baby isn't here yet," said Sal. "Alex said for a couple of us to go and check on the man we left tied up and see if he has been found. He said to be careful and don't go in if he has been found. If he hasn't been found, he wants us to move him so the others won't know what happened to him."

Sandy stood and looked at the others. "Andrew if you can stay here with Bobby, I'll go and get Minnie and Sal and Micky can go and check on the man we left tied up."

Andrew sat down and the others headed out the door. Sal left the key to the apartment on the table inside the door and they took the elevator down to the third floor. The elevator did not go to the garage. They had to take another elevator down from there.

Lynn glanced up when they appeared. "How's Bobby?" she asked.

"He's going to be alright," said Sal. "They broke all the fingers on his right hand."

Lynn winced. "They wanted to stop him from writing."

"Yeah," agreed Sandy. "They didn't want him able to file the story. What they didn't know is Bobby is left handed."

Lynn and the others smiled. "Haven't they ever heard of a voice recorder?" asked Lynn.

"I don't think they are the smartest people. If they were smart, they would not be breaking the law when they are supposed to be upholding it," said Micky.

They all agreed as the guys entered the elevator to the garage.

THREE

AFTER SANDY AND SAL LEFT, Minnie looked around Sandy's room. She walked around and looked at his pictures on his dresser. There were pictures of his parents and some pictures of Sandy and Sal at different ages. There was a picture of them with Bobby when they were teenagers. Minnie was startled when she saw a picture of her at her sixteenth birthday.

"I guess he must like me a little," she said.

"Of course, he does, he is your true love," said her guardian angel.

"Maybe he will realize I'm not a little girl anymore," said Minnie.

"I'm sure he is well aware of that fact," observed her guardian angel.

Minnie frowned. "How can you be so sure?" she asked.

"I talked to his guardian angel. He said Sandy has very strong feelings for you. It is up to us to be sure the two of you are aware of your love and help you and Sandy figure out your feelings," said her guardian angel.

"Thank you for watching out for me and helping me to get away from Arnie and his friends," said Minnie.

"I will always look after you and help you stay safe," said her guardian angel.

"Thanks, I felt a lot better just knowing I wasn't alone," said Minnie.

"Why don't you take a shower and try to take a nap until Sandy gets back?" suggested her guardian angel.

"I don't feel like taking a shower right now. I think I will lie down for a while. I haven't been resting well for a while," said Minnie.

She went over to Sandy's bed and sat on the edge. She took off her shoes and lay back and stretched out. She pulled out his pillow and held it close to her face. It smelled like Sandy. She held it close and snuggled down in the bed with the pillow held close in her arms. Minnie was soon sleeping soundly.

She was still sleeping when Sandy quietly let himself into the apartment. He was there to take her to Bobby. He looked around the apartment; but saw no sign of Minnie. He went to his room and tapped lightly on the door. When there was no answer, he opened the door and looked inside.

Sandy smiled to see Minnie on his bed snuggled up to his pillow sleeping soundly. He walked over to the bed and stood looked down at her.

"She is where she belongs," thought Sandy.

"You need to let her know how you feel about her. It will be the best way to keep her safe," said his guardian angel.

"I don't want to take advantage of her," said Sandy softly.

Minnie stirred at the sound of his voice. She opened her eyes and looked up at him and smiled.

Sandy smiled back at her. "I didn't mean to wake you," he said.

Minnie took his hand and rubbed her cheek against it. "I had a nice nap. I rested better than I have in a while.

Sandy frowned at the reminder of why she was here, sleeping in his bed.

"We found Bobby. He's in rough shape. The doctor said he is

mostly bruised and dehydrated except for his fingers, which were broken. He's resting, but I can take you to see him."

"Thank you," said Minnie sitting up and putting her shoes on.

Sandy put his arms around her and pulled her close.

"He's not awake, but I thought you would feel better if you could see him," said Sandy.

Minnie looked up into his face. "Yes, I would," she agreed.

Sandy guided her out with his arm still around her. "Is he in the hospital?" she asked.

"No, we took him to Avorn Security. We did not want Arnie and his friends to get their hands on him again," said Sandy. Minnie nodded agreement.

They went out through the kitchen into the garage. Sandy picked up Minnie's backpack on the way and brought it along with them.

"You need to bend down so you can't be seen, just in case someone is watching," said Sandy. Minnie obediently slid down in the seat so she wouldn't be seen. Sandy put her backpack in the floor at her feet before closing the door.

When they were away from the house, and Sandy was sure he wasn't being followed, he told her she could sit up. Minnie scooted up in her seat and looked around. She was quiet as Sandy drove to the Avorn Security building and into their garage.

Sandy helped her out and took her backpack from her before leading her into the elevator. Brenda looked up and smiled at Minnie when they arrived on the third floor.

"Where is Lynn?" asked Sandy

"She had to take a few days off to take care of her mother," said Brenda. "I'm filling in for her."

"Is her mother alright?" asked Sandy.

"I think so, she just needs to stay off of her feet for a few days," said Brenda.

Brenda stood and came over and took Minnie's hand. "I'm Brenda, Alex's assistant. I'm sorry about your brother, but if you need anything while you are here, let me know, and I will take care of it."

Minnie was startled, but she squeezed her hand and smiled back at her. "Thank you," she said.

"Has Alex checked in?" asked Sandy.

Brenda smiled at him. "Yes, Lori and Trey's little girl is finally here. Mother and baby are both doing fine and taking a nap," said Brenda.

Sandy smiled widely. "Great," he said. He took Minnie's hand to lead her to another elevator. "We need to get to Bobby. We'll see you later," said Sandy. Brenda waved them on as she returned to her seat and resumed her work.

Sandy knocked on the door of 602. It was opened by Andrew. He smiled at Minnie, and she smiled back at him.

"Minnie this is Andrew. He is keeping an eye on Bobby," said Sandy. "Andrew this is Bobby's sister, Minnie."

"It's nice to meet you, Minnie," said Andrew.

"Thank you for looking after my brother," said Minnie.

"How is Bobby doing?" asked Sandy.

"He is still sleeping. The nurse came with more IV bags. She is in with Bobby now," said Andrew.

Andrew closed the door as Sandy guided Minnie to Bobby's room with his arm still around her.

Minnie was grateful for the feeling of support Sandy's closeness gave her.

"I told you he had feelings for you. You two are meant to be together," said her guardian angel.

"We'll discuss this later," thought Minnie.

Minnie glanced at the nurse and nodded hello, but she gave a gasp as Sandy led her to Bobby's bedside, and she got her first good look at her brother. They stood beside his bed and Minnie looked down at a Bobby who was almost unrecognizable. He was covered with bruises, and his hand was in a cast with his fingers separated by splints.

Minnie felt her eyes misting over and blinked them away. She reached out a hand and gently pushed his hair back off his forehead. With a sob, she turned and buried her face in Sandy's chest.

Sandy held her close and rubbed a soothing hand over her back.

"He is going to be alright," said Sandy.

Minnie pulled back slightly and looked up at Sandy. "Thank you, guys for going to find him and getting him away from Arnie and his goons before they killed him," said Minnie.

"You are welcome. He is our friend. Of course, we had to save him. He would have done the same for us. I wish he had come to us for help before he was in over his head," said Sandy.

Minnie looked at Bobby thoughtfully.

"Why didn't his guardian angel warn him before he was taken?" Minnie asked her guardian angel.

"He was warned, but he didn't listen. He was so determined to get evidence on his stepfather and break the story on the corruption, he just closed himself off from his guardian angel," Minnie's guardian angel replied.

"What is it?" asked Sandy sensing Minnie's distraction.

"I was asking why his guardian angel didn't warn him," said Minnie looking up at Sandy.

"Did she say why?" asked Sandy.

"She said Bobby shut his guardian angel out and didn't listen to the warning. He was so determined to get the evidence on Arnie, he ignored his guardian angel," said Minnie.

"That sounds like Bobby," said Sandy. "Let's go into the living room and let the nurse take care of Bobby."

"Okay," said Minnie holding on to Sandy's hand as he led her back into the front room.

"Are you sure Mom is going to be alright with Arnie?" asked Minnie.

"I can't be absolutely sure, but I think he is keeping his real character hidden from her for now. We will have to keep an eye on her and hope we can get Arnie and his friends behind bars before they hurt anyone else," said Sandy.

Andrew was listening to them as they came into the living room.

"I could go over and keep an eye on Minnie's mom," said Andrew. "I am not needed here since the nurse is keeping an eye on Bobby."

"Alex and Mariam should be back soon. Why don't we wait and see what he wants us to do?" said Sandy.

"Okay," agreed Andrew with a nod. He turned back to the TV screens that were lined up on the wall in front of the couch. He pointed the remote at one and Minnie gasped as she saw down the hall and watched Sal and Micky leave the elevator and start toward their door. Andrew rose and went to open the door for them.

"I wasn't expecting you back so soon," said Sandy as Sal and Micky entered the apartment.

"About a block from the building, my guardian angel told me we were headed for a trap, so we parked and watched for a while. We saw some police cars pass on their way to the abandoned factory. They had their lights and sirens on and were going fast; so, when they passed, we left and came here," said Sal.

"I wonder what is going on," said Sandy. "Andrew see if there are any news reports."

Andrew pointed the remote at a different TV screen and the news channel came on. The news vans and reporters were gathered around the front of the abandoned building.

"We are here at the scene of the murder of a policeman. He was found tied to a chair with a bullet hole in his head. The police are not saying anything about the case. They are gathering evidence and trying to find out why one of our law enforcement officers would be in such a place. Stay tuned, we will have updates as they are available."

Sal cursed and looked at the others. "Why would they shoot their own man?" he asked.

"He may have been shot by the people they were taking payoffs from," said Micky.

The others nodded agreement.

"I hope Alex has been in touch with the FBI. We don't know who we can trust at the local police department," said Sal.

Minnie snuggled closer to Sandy, and he tightened his arm around her.

Sal looked over and smiled at her. "I'm glad you are here with us," said Sal.

"Me, too," agreed Minnie.

There was a knock at the door, and Andrew went to open it and let Alex and Mariam in.

The guys looked surprised to see Mariam with Alex, but she just smiled at their startled expressions.

"We just came from the hospital and Mariam wanted to be sure Bobby was alright," said Alex.

"Beside broken fingers, he is going to be okay. He is sleeping. I think the doctor wants him to sleep as long as he can so he can heal,' said Sal.

Mariam came over and took Minnie's hand. "I'm Mariam. You must be Minnie. I'm sorry we have to meet under such conditions, but it is nice to meet you."

Minnie smiled at Mariam. "Thank you, thank all of you for helping Bobby and me," said Minnie.

Mariam smiled. "My guardian angel said you are going to be an important part of our group, so we have to take care of our own," said Mariam.

The guys looked startled at her remarks. Even Alex looked at her curiously; and smiled at Minnie. He watched how protective Sandy was of Minnie and nodded his understanding.

"What is the latest news?" asked Alex.

"Someone shot the policeman we left tied up at the abandoned factory building," said Sal. "We don't know who did the shooting. It was on the news. We didn't make it back to the building to check on him. My guardian angel warned me not to go there."

Alex nodded. "I'm glad you listened. We don't need to be tied into this situation in the minds of the local police. I have forwarded the information you sent me to my FBI contacts, and we will let them take care of the corrupt policeman unless some of our own are in danger, or we are asked for help."

All of the men nodded agreement and Sal turned toward the kitchen.

"I don't know about the rest of you, but I am hungry, and I have a piece of chocolate cake with my name on it," said Sal.

"I didn't know you brought your mom's cake with you," said Micky as he turned and followed Sal out.

Andrew looked at Alex as if waiting for instructions.

Mariam took Minnie's hand and led her over to the sofa to sit beside her. "I know you are worried about your mom. We will have to figure out a way to help her. Since Lori and Trey's little girl is here maybe he will be able to help us," said Mariam.

"How can he help?" asked Minnie.

"Trey can talk to our guardian angels and, with their help, he can reprogram people like your stepfather so they will not be a danger to anyone anymore," said Mariam.

"Sometimes he can," said Alex. "It doesn't always work. Sometimes people are so far removed from their guardian angels. They can't be helped," said Alex.

"I didn't know anyone could talk to other people's guardian angels. I just depend on mine to find out what is going on and tell me," said Minnie.

"Have you had any trouble with witch hunters thinking you are a witch, because you can communicate with your guardian angel?" asked Mariam.

"No, Mom told me to keep quiet about talking to my guardian angel. She said most people wouldn't believe me, or they would hurt me," said Minnie. "Mom had an aunt almost burned as a witch when she was very young. Her parents moved her and her two brothers away from the town where they had been living and didn't tell anyone where they moved to. They even changed their name."

Mariam nodded. "My parents and my younger brother died

when someone used the witch hunters to get to my father's money. They burned our house. My older brother and I were not there at the time, but they were still trying to get to me. Alex and the guys saved me and reprogrammed the witch hunters. We haven't had any problems with them lately, but we stay alert."

Minnie gazed at her wide eyed. "You must have been furious," she said.

Mariam smiled. "Most people didn't understand that even though I was scared and running for my life, I was furious anyone would take it upon their selves to decide if my family or I deserved to live," said Mariam.

"I am glad you are okay," said Minnie.

"I am fine, and we are going to make sure you are fine, too, said Mariam.

Alex had been listening to them while talking to Andrew and Sandy.

"I am sending for the key to the apartment next door. Andrew is going to stay here and keep an eye on Bobby and the nurse. You and Sandy can stay in 601. I'm going to send Sal and Micky out to keep an eye on your house. Do you have a job?" he asked.

"Yes, I work in a day care, but I have a few days off. I was worried about Bobby and I took a few days off to see if I could find him," said Minnie.

"Good, we just have to come up with an excuse to give your mom for your absence," said Alex.

"I told her I was spending the night with my friend Louanne," said Minnie.

"Good," said Alex. "We will worry about tomorrow later," he said with a smile

FOUR

ALEX AND MARIAM left after Mariam gave Minnie a hug; and assured her they were going to be friends and if she needed anything to have one of the guys call her. She promised Minnie she would see her soon.

Brenda sent the key to 601 up to 602. Minnie took a last look at Bobby before allowing Sandy to show her the apartment next door.

"Are you hungry?" asked Sandy. "We can order some food sent up from the restaurant downstairs."

"You have a restaurant downstairs?" asked Minnie in surprise.

"Yes, it is on the first floor. It is open to the public. I'll have to give you a tour of the building in a few days when we can be sure you are safe," said Sandy.

"I'd like that," agreed Minnie.

"You didn't say if you are hungry," said Sandy.

Minnie smiled. "I am a little hungry. I haven't had much appetite lately. I have been so worried about Bobby."

"Would you like anything in particular?" asked Sandy.

"No, surprise me," said Minnie.

Sandy went over to the panel by the door and pushed the button for the restaurant.

"Hello," answered a voice.

"Hello, Lee, this is Sandy Mase. Would you send up two of today's specials to Brenda on the third floor?"

"Sure, they will be right there," said Lee.

"Thanks," said Sandy letting go of the button. He then pushed the button with Brenda's name on it. When Brenda answered, he told her to expect the food and to send it to 601.

Minnie was sitting watching him in amazement. "You guys are spoiled," she said.

Sandy smiled and came over and sat next to her on the sofa.

"We have to keep these apartments safe. Sometimes Alex has some important visitors staying here, and he assures their safety. It also provides an extra level of security for him and Mariam. They have the penthouse apartment on the seventh floor. They have their own private elevator and a staircase between the sixth and seventh floor. The door between the two floors is locked and Alex and Mariam have the only keys.

"Isn't that dangerous? What if there is a fire?" asked Minnie.

"There is a release control in the penthouse." said Sandy. "Alex can open the door or unlock the elevator to the penthouse from there."

Minnie shook her head. "It's nice, but I'll be glad when I can live in a regular house without worrying about anyone coming after me," she said.

Sandy looked at her and smiled in complete agreement.

There was a knock at the door and Sandy opened the door to take their food from Brenda's messenger.

"Whatever it is, it smells great," said Minnie.

Sandy took the food into the kitchen and put the bags on the counter. Minnie followed him in and sat on a stool at the counter. Sandy opened the bag and took out two covered plates and several accessories. He placed them in front of the two stools. One was in front of Minnie.

"Is tea okay to drink?" asked Sandy.

"Yes, thank you," said Minnie.

Sandy fixed two glasses of tea and set them on the counter. One was in front of Minnie.

Minnie took the cover off her plate and gazed in amazement at the beautifully arranged food. There was a large slice of meatloaf, mashed potatoes with butter, green beans and glazed carrots. There was a roll included and a large slice of lemon meringue pie.

Minnie sat looking at her plate enjoying the colors and smelling how good it smelled.

Sandy grinned as he watched her. He picked up his fork and took a bite. "Dig in. It really is delicious," he said.

Minnie grinned at him as she took her first bite. "Ummmm," she said. "It really does taste as good as it looks."

They were silent as the food melted away. Minnie placed her fork on her plate and leaned back as she gazed at the large slice of pie.

"I am so full. I think I will have to wait awhile before eating my pie," she said.

Sandy grinned at her as he finished his own plate and decided to wait and have his pie later also. "We can have a dessert break before bed," he said.

They covered the desserts and started stacking their other dishes and cleaning up the counter. They took the plates and utensils to the sink and washed them before putting them back in the bags to be returned downstairs.

"How do we get them back downstairs?" asked Minnie.

"We will return them in the morning when they send up break-fast," replied Sandy. "I didn't want them to be sitting around dirty all night."

Minnie nodded her agreement.

"Do you want to watch a show on the TV?" asked Sandy.

"Sure," agreed Minnie. "Thanks for the food. It was great."

"Yes, it was. Don't tell Mom, but their food is almost as good as hers," said Sandy with a smile.

Minnie looked at him and smiled. "I won't tell," she promised.

Sandy picked up the remote and joined Minnie on the sofa. He sat close to her and pointed the remote at the TV.

"Let's see if we can find something to watch," remarked Sandy.

Minnie looked up at Sandy and snuggled closer to his side. She didn't care what they watched so long as she could sit close to Sandy and watch it.

"I told you he had feelings for you," said her guardian angel.

"I know you did. Now, let me enjoy being with him," thought Minnie.

Sandy looked down at her and smiled. He was right where he wanted to be. He had given up hope of ever being this close to Minnie.

"You need to let her know how you feel about her," said his guardian angel.

"I will, just let me enjoy her company while I have the chance," thought Sandy.

"You would have a lot of chances if you would just let her know your feelings for her," argued his guardian angel.

Sandy looked down at Minnie again and smiled when he found her looking up at him.

"Do you have anything you would like to watch on TV?" asked Sandy.

"I don't care as long as I can sit here beside you and feel safe while we watch it," said Minnie.

Sandy's smile faded. "Was she just with him to feel safe?" he asked himself.

"Of course, she feels safe with you," said his guardian angel in exasperation. "She has feelings for you." Sandy frowned.

"What's wrong?" asked Minnie seeing his change of expression.

"What?" said Sandy looking down at her startled from his conversation with his guardian angel?

"Why are you frowning?" asked Minnie.

"I was just thinking about something," said Sandy.

Minnie laid her head on his chest. "Well stop thinking about whatever it is. I don't get many chances to enjoy being with you, and I want to know you are enjoying being with me, too," said Minnie.

"Of course, I am enjoying being with you. I have been waiting for you to grow up, so I could let you know how I have felt about you for years," said Sandy.

Minnie sat up and smiled at Sandy. "If your feelings are anything like mine have been for years, I think you should know I am grown up enough, and I am tired of waiting to let you know how I feel about you."

Sandy drew her closer in his arms and grinned. "You have feelings for me?" he asked. Minnie nodded. "Great," said Sandy as he leaned in and kissed her.

Minnie kissed him back, and the kiss deepened. When they finally came up for air; they sat, with their foreheads touching and their arms tight around each other, breathing deeply.

"How long have you had feelings for me?" asked Minnie, when she could speak again.

Sandy smiled at her. "I always felt like I had to keep you safe when you followed us around, but it was on your sixteenth birthday I realized my feelings were deeper. I knew you were too young, and Bobby would have beaten the crap out of me if I made any move toward you, so I tried to wait, patiently, for you to grow up."

"I am glad our wait is over," said Minnie. "My guardian angel has been encouraging me to tell you how I felt, but I wasn't sure if you felt the same."

"My guardian angel has been pushing me to tell you my feelings. Do you think they have been trying to get us together?" asked Sandy.

"I wouldn't be surprised," said Minnie with a grin. "My guardian angel informed me one of their most important duties is to help their charges find their true loves."

Sandy rubbed his hand over her head and gently pushed her hair back off of her face. "I am glad they are with us. I am also glad to know you are my true love." Sandy frowned. "We just have to take care of Arnie and his friends so we can start building a life together."

"Yes," agreed Minnie as she raised her face for another kiss. She had been waiting long enough for this. She was not going to let thoughts of Arnie and his friends spoil the moment for her and Sandy.

They continued to kiss and talk to each other. The TV played in the background, but it was ignored by them.

It was late when Sandy sat up and pulled back from Minnie. "We need to get some sleep," he said kissing her lightly.

Minnie squeezed him tightly. "I don't want to let you go. I'm afraid I'll wake up and find out I have been dreaming and this never happened."

Sandy smiled down into her eyes. "This is no dream and I will be here when you wake up. If you need me, I'll be close by. If you call, I'll hear you and be by your side at once. We can leave our doors open so we can hear each other better," said Sandy.

Minnie reluctantly let Sandy help her to stand and after one last kiss, Minnie went into her room to try and get some sleep.

Sandy watched her go and sat back down on the sofa. He leaned back and smiled when he thought Minnie.

"She loves me," he thought to his guardian angel.

"I told you. You should listen to me," said his guardian angel.

"I'm too happy to argue with you right now, so I'll just agree with you and promise to listen more closely to what you say from now on," thought Sandy.

Minnie was having a similar conversation with her guardian angel as she thanked her for letting her know about Sandy's feelings. She dug through her backpack and pulled out a tee shirt to sleep in. After changing clothes, Minnie climbed into bed and closed her eyes. She thought she was too excited to get to sleep, but, was sound asleep in minutes.

Sandy looked in on her and smiled when he found her sleeping.

He went into his room and lie down and fell asleep almost as fast as Minnie.

Minnie awakened first the next morning. She lay there for a while thinking about Sandy and smiling. Finally, she got out of bed and dressed so she could go to the bathroom. She tried to be quiet so she would not wake Sandy, but he heard her stirring around and was awake instantly.

When Sandy realized Minnie was in the bathroom, he went to the kitchen and turned the coffee maker on. He had prepared it the night before.

"Good morning," said Sandy as Minnie emerged from the bathroom.

Minnie smiled at his greeting.

"Good morning, I didn't mean to wake you up," she said as she went to him and reached for a kiss.

Sandy put his arms around her.

"This is the perfect way to start the day," he said and kissed her again.

"Perfect," agreed Minnie. "Is there any news?" asked Minnie.

"I haven't talked to anyone this morning," said Sandy. "Would you like some coffee?"

"Yes please, with cream and sugar," said Minnie.

Sandy poured two cups of coffee and sat the sugar bowl on the counter. He took a small container of cream from the refrigerator and placed it on the counter also.

Minnie stirred the sugar and creamer into her coffee and took a drink. "This is good," she said.

Sandy smiled at her as he drank his own coffee black and straight. "What do you want to order for breakfast?" he asked.

"Something light, I am not very hungry, and I want to check on Bobby," said Minnie.

"I'm sure he is fine. If there had been any change, Andrew would have called us," said Sandy as he went over and ordered their breakfast.

"I feel guilty about not letting Mom know about Bobby being hurt," said Minnie looking down and frowning.

Sandy put his arms around her and pulled her close.

"I know, but we can't take a chance with Arnie in the picture. Your mom trusts him, and she would tell him about us, and we would all be in danger," said Sandy.

"I know," agreed Minnie. "I won't say anything. I just hope this whole thing can be solved without anyone else getting hurt."

"I hope so, too," agreed Sandy. "We can trust Alex to figure things out. He has gotten us all out of some tight spots before."

"He sounds like a good person to have on our side," said Minnie.

"Yes, he is," agreed Sandy. "The best." Sandy pulled back and smiled at her.

"I'm going to take a quick shower before our food arrives," he said giving her a quick kiss and heading for the bathroom. "If the doorbell rings, don't answer it. They will leave our food by the door."

He turned back and took the bag with the dishes from the night before and placed them outside the door.

When he came back by Minnie, he stole another quick kiss before going into the bathroom.

Minnie smiled as she made her way over to the sofa and reached for the TV remote. She studied the remote and saw a button marked TV and pushed it. She smiled as one of the screens lit up.

The news was on and the news person was standing in front of the police station.

"The police have said the execution style slaying of Police Officer Kane was the result of his cover being blown. Officer Kane had been under cover for about a year, gathering evidence on drug traffickers. The police do not know how his cover was blown, but the investigation is ongoing." The reporter sent the news back to the station and other news.

Minnie frowned and leaned back on the sofa. She was no longer listening to the news,

"They are going to cover up his breaking the law," she said. "Someone is covering for him."

"What?" asked Sandy as he emerged from the bathroom.

"They were just talking about the police officer who was shot. They are covering for him, claiming he was working under cover and he was killed because his cover was blown," said Minnie.

Sandy frowned. "We are going to have to be careful who we talk to. It sounds like they are trying to cover the police department. To make themselves look good, they will whitewash him," said Sandy.

Minnie looked at Sandy. "I don't care what they say. I heard them talking, and they were not doing anything for anyone but themselves."

"I know," agreed Sandy. "I'm the one who cut Bobby out of that chair. There is no way they could have been working undercover." Minnie nodded her agreement.

The doorbell rang, and Sandy went to open the door and take delivery of their breakfast.

"Come and eat," said Sandy after closing the door and heading for the kitchen. Minnie followed behind him. The smell coming from the bags had awakened her appetite.

FIVE

AFTER BREAKFAST MINNIE and Sandy went next door to check on Bobby. Andrew let them in when Sandy knocked on the door.

"How is Bobby?" asked Minnie.

"He is the same. He hasn't awakened, yet," said Andrew.

"Have you seen the news?" asked Sandy.

"Yes, I saw it earlier. Alex saw it, too. He will be over here soon. He wants to talk about the story the police department is putting out," said Andrew.

Minnie left them talking and went to Bobby's room to check on him. She went in and quietly stood at his bedside. The nurse joined her there.

"He is doing fine," said the nurse. "The doctor will be by to check on him later this morning."

Minnie smiled at her and thanked her before returning to the living room and joining Sandy. Sandy put an arm around her when she stopped at his side.

"Would you like some coffee," asked Andrew.

"No, thank you," said Minnie. "We just had coffee with breakfast."

There was a knock at the door and Andrew went to open the door for Alex.

"Good morning," said Alex as he entered.

"Good morning," all three responded.

Alex looked at Minnie and smiled. "I'm glad to see you looking more rested," he said.

"I feel much better," said Minnie smiling back and holding tightly to Sandy's hand.

Alex went over to the counter and poured himself a cup of coffee. "I heard back from my FBI contact. They are investigating the police corruption, but he said they would have a hard time proving it if the police continue with their story of undercover work. It gives the policemen an alibi for everything they were doing and provides them a cover story," said Alex.

"They are going to get away with everything," said Andrew disgusted.

Alex shook his head. "It is not over, yet," he said. "We still have several options."

"What options?" asked Sandy.

"We will wait and see what the FBI and the police department do. If they don't take care of the problem, we will see if Trey can reprogram the bad guys." He shook his head and held up his hand when Sandy and Andrew started to speak. "I know it would be better if they paid for their crimes, but at least Minnie and Bobby would be safe, and they wouldn't be hurting anyone else."

"What do you mean, reprogram them?" asked Minnie.

"Trey can talk to their guardian angels and have the guardian angels change the men's memories," said Alex.

"Wow! I didn't know anyone could do that," said Minnie.

"It doesn't always work, but we can try. It will be a few days before Trey will be able to work on them. He is at the hospital with Lori and Crystal," said Alex.

"They named the baby Crystal," said Andrew with a grin.

"It is a pretty name," said Minnie. Sandy grinned down at her and nodded his agreement.

"Her name is Crystal Lorraine Loden. They named her after Lori," said Alex with a smile.

Alex stood up. "I need to go and see if Mariam has awakened, yet. I'll let you know if I hear anything else. Minnie, you need to stay here and think up a story to tell your mom about not returning home for a few days."

"Okay," agreed Minnie.

Alex left and Minnie turned to Sandy. His arms closed around her and she snuggled close to him. Andrew took the remote and started checking out different TV screens.

"I feel so guilty about not letting Mom know about Bobby and lying to her about where I am," said Minnie.

"I know," agreed Sandy. "Maybe we will get things straightened out soon, and you can tell her what is going on."

"She has worked so hard for years to make a life for us. Even now, even though she is married to Arnie, she still works full time at the school," said Minnie. "I asked her when she first married Arnie if she was going to quit her job. She said she did not marry Arnie for him to pay her way. She married him because she loved him. She said she had been taking care of herself and us for a long time, and she would continue to do so as long as she was able." Minnie looked up at Sandy and smiled. "Mom is a very independent person."

"I know," agreed Sandy. "I like your mom. She always treated me and Sal just like Bobby. She would bake us cookies on her days off, and she never yelled at us when we got into mischief."

Minnie smiled. "When did you get into mischief?"

"We found this stray dog one time. Bobby got down a large pan, and we were giving it a bath in the kitchen at your house. The dog got away from us, and we were chasing it all around the living room and kitchen trying to get it back in the water to finish its bath. It was knocking things over, and we were getting water all over the floor. Your mom came in, she had been grocery shopping, and you were with her. She stopped in her tracks, right inside the door. She looked around, and we thought we were in for it, but she just looked at us, then she looked at the dog. She pointed her finger at him and sternly told him to get back in the pan of water. When she pointed her finger at the pan of water, the dog put his tail between his legs and slunk over to the pan and climbed in. He sat there looking at your mom as if asking 'what now?'"

Sandy shook his head and laughed. "Your mom walked over to the pantry and got a broom and a dustpan. She handed them to Bobby. She gave me a mop, and she told Sal to finish giving the dog a bath. While we were cleaning, she ignored us and had you helping her put away the groceries. When we were finished and had emptied the pan of water outside, she had us wash our hands and sat us down at the table with glasses of milk and cookies. She never fussed at us at all,"

Sandy looked at Minnie who was laughing at his story.

"I remember when we got Smiley," said Minnie still laughing. "I remember the mess, too. Mom was smiling to herself all the time we were putting away the groceries. She made sure not to let you boys see her. When I asked her about it later, she said you boys were showing compassion for a homeless animal. She said you boys needed him to take care of as much as he needed you to take care of him. She said it was a good growing up experience for all of you. I didn't really understand then, but Smiley became a member of the family. He loved Mom. She only had to tell him something and he scrambled to please her. She loved him, too. We were all sad when he died. We even had a funeral for him." Minnie wasn't laughing anymore. She turned her face into Sandy, and he held her close.

"Yeah, Bobby and I gathered all of the wildflowers we could find to put on his grave," said Sandy.

"It was beautiful," agreed Minnie smiling up at Sandy again.

Andrew looked over at them and smiled. "Did you guys ever get another pet?" asked Andrew.

"No," said Sandy. "We were graduating high school when Smiley died, and our parents told us we were not around enough to give a pet the care and attention it needed. They told us to wait until we settled down before getting another pet."

"Maybe when this is all settled, we can get us a dog," said Minnie looking up at Sandy.

"Maybe we will," agreed Sandy giving her a quick kiss.

Andrew grinned and turned back to the TV screens. He started switching from one to the other checking out the other floors in the building.

"What do we have here?" said Andrew.

He was looking at the hall on the third floor and watching two policemen get out of the elevator and approach Brenda. Brenda smiled asked if she could help them. Andrew turned on the sound so they could listen to the reply.

"We need to see Alex Avorn," said one of the policemen.

"Do you have an appointment?" asked Brenda.

"We don't have to have an appointment. Now get your boss down here," snarled the other policeman.

Brenda gave him a stern look and started to speak, but, stopped when the elevator door opened, and Alex exited.

"It's okay, Brenda," said Alex.

Alex looked at the policeman, who had spoken to Brenda.

"You are in my building and if I ever hear you talk to one of my employees like you just did, I will have you escorted from this building, and you will never enter it again," said Alex.

The policeman looked away and his partner spoke to Alex. "We are sorry for the misunderstanding, Mr. Avorn. The chief asked us to come and talk to you. We would appreciate it if you could spare us a few minutes of your time," he said.

Alex looked at them for a minute, then, he nodded. "Of course. What can I do for you?"

"Now, what did the chief want you to ask me about?" asked Alex. He leaned casually against the desk.

"My name is Collin Weldon and this is Malcomb Clark," said Collin. "We had a policeman murdered yesterday."

"I saw the report on the news," said Alex.

'The chief is worried it will look bad if we do the investigation. He thinks we might be accused of covering up something. He wanted to know if you would be interested in looking into the matter for the police department."

Alex looked startled. He studied both men. "I will think about it and call the chief and talk to him before I make up my mind," said Alex.

Collin turned toward Alex and held out his hand. "Thank you for seeing us. I'll let the chief know you will be calling."

Alex shook his hand and watched as they entered the elevator and it started down. Alex leaned over Brenda's desk and pushed a button.

"Frank, keep an eye out for those two policemen and make sure they leave the building," said Alex.

"Sure thing, Boss," said Frank at the front security desk.

Alex turned and looked at Brenda.

"Are you alright?" he asked.

Brenda smiled. "I'm fine. I can handle a bullying cop any day," she said.

"You don't have to. If it happens again, push the button for security and have them escorted from the building," said Alex.

"Aye, Aye, Boss," said Brenda saluting.

Alex just smiled and shook his head as he started for his elevator.

Andrew, Sandy, and Minnie turned from watching the monitor for the third floor.

"I'm sure glad Alex is on my side," said Minnie. "Those officers switched their tone fast after he talked to them."

"Yes," agreed Sandy. "Alex makes a very good friend and a first class employer. He is always fair and doesn't stand for any nonsense."

"He will go the limit for what he believes in," agreed Andrew.

Minnie squeezed Sandy's hand.

"I think I will go and sit with Bobby for a while," she said.

Sandy hugged her before, reluctantly letting her go.

"Be thinking about something we can tell your mom about why you need to stay away from home for a few days," said Sandy.

Minnie nodded. "I'll try to think of something."

Sandy was quiet as he watched Minnie go into Bobby's room and take a seat at his bedside. He sighed as he turned back to Andrew.

"Have you heard anything from Sal and Micky?" asked Sandy.

"They called earlier. Minnie's mom has left for work, and she had been gone about thirty minutes when one of Arnie's friends showed up. Sal said they have been quiet. He thinks they are trying to avoid drawing attention to themselves because their buddy was shot," said Andrew.

"Yeah, they could be in big trouble if the chief started looking in their direction," agreed Sandy.

Minnie took Bobby's hand and held it gently.

"You have to wake up and talk to us Bobby. I miss having my big brother bossing me around. You are going to have to work on this problem you have with staying safe. Sandy and Sal helped save you. They are making sure you are safe and have a chance to heal," Minnie sighed. "I'm telling you right now, I'm in love with Sandy. He loves me, too. If you have a problem with it, you will just have to get over it. I have been in love with Sandy for a long time, and I am not letting anyone come between us, even you, big brother.

"My guardian angel has been telling me for ages that Sandy loved me, too, but I was afraid to take a chance. I am so glad I finally listened. If you had listened to your guardian angel, you would not be in this bed recovering from being almost killed. You know your guardian angel will look after you, but you have to pay attention. Oh, Bobby, please think about all the people who love you before you head into danger again."

Minnie stopped talking and wiped the tears from her eyes. She squeezed Bobby's hand and rose from her seat.

When she went back into the living room, Sandy was waiting and drew her close. He didn't say anything, just held her. Minnie looked up at him with drenched eyes. Sandy leaned down and kissed her gently. "He's going to be alright," said Sandy.

"I know," agreed Minnie. "It's just so hard seeing all the bruises and knowing how he was tortured."

The nurse opened the door to the other bedroom and joined them. "Good morning," she said. "Has my patient awakened, yet?"

"I was just in there," said Minnie. "He is still sleeping."

The nurse patted her arm. "Don't worry. Sleep is the best thing for him right now. If he was awake, he would be in a lot of pain. Sleep gives him a chance to heal some without hurting so much."

Minnie smiled. "I hadn't thought about it like that. I just wanted him to open his eyes and tell me he was okay."

The nurse smiled. "He will soon. Is there any coffee around here?"

Andrew quickly came over and smiling, led her to the kitchen where he had a fresh pot of coffee brewing.

Sandy and Minnie smiled at each other as they watched them go. "Have you thought about what you can tell your mom?" asked Sandy. Minnie sighed and went over to the sofa and sat down. Sandy followed her over and sat beside her.

"I have been thinking, but so far I haven't decided what I can tell her. She knows I have time off. She also knows I have been saving money so I can take some college classes. I thought I might tell her I was visiting campuses to check them out and see where I wanted to go. I don't know if she will accept it as a reason for not being at home. I'm pretty sure Arnie will be suspicious, especially since you guys rescued Bobby."

"Don't worry about Arnie," said Sandy. "We will be taking care of him before too long. He won't be a problem for you or your mom."

Minnie shivered. She turned her face into Sandy's side and snuggled closer to him. "I hope you are right," she said.

"I am always right," teased Sandy with a grin.

"I think I will have my guardian angel check with your guardian angel about that," said Minnie grinning up at him.

"I'll have to have a talk with my guardian angel and make sure he doesn't rat me out," said Sandy.

Minnie laughed, "I don't think you have anything to worry about. Both of our guardian angels are determined to keep us together. They are not going to do anything to keep us apart."

"I'm glad they are on our side," said Sandy.

"Me, too," agreed Minnie raising her face for another kiss. Sandy was happy to oblige her.

SIX

MINNIE AND SANDY were interrupted when Minnie's phone rang. Minnie looked at the screen and, when she saw Louanne's name, quickly said hello.

"Hey," said Louanne.

"Has my mom called you?" asked Minnie.

"No, she hasn't called, but I wanted to let you know Cathy, Sari, and I are heading out tomorrow to scout some colleges. We want to see which ones we like best," said Louanne.

"I was just thinking about checking out the campuses myself." said Minnie.

"Do you want to come with us?" asked Louanne.

"I'll let you know. Will you let your mom know I'm thinking of going with you?" asked Minnie.

"Sure," laughed Louanne. "I'll tell her you are going with us, just in case your mom calls."

"I don't think she will, but my stepdad might push her to check up on me. I don't want him getting any ideas," said Minnie.

"Is he giving you a hard time?" asked Louanne seriously.

"I'll handle him. Don't worry," said Minnie.

"Okay, keep in touch," said Louanne.

"I will. Thanks for helping," said Minnie as she hung up her phone and looked at Sandy, who had been sitting quietly listening.

Minnie smiled at him. "Louanne and a couple of our friends are leaving tomorrow to tour some college campuses," said Minnie. "Now, if I can convince my mom I am going with them, it will solve the problem of why I am not going home."

Minnie started to call her mom, but when she glanced at the time.

"I need to wait and call her at work," she said.

'Are you hungry?" asked Sandy.

"No, I'm still full from breakfast," replied Minnie.

Sandy stood and took her hand and helped her up. "We can take a look around the building while you are waiting to call your mom," said Sandy.

"Okay," agreed Minnie.

Sandy went into the kitchen to let Andrew know he was going to show Minnie around the building. When he returned, he smiled and took Minnie's hand again to guide her out of the apartment. They entered the elevator and went down to the fifth floor.

When the elevator door opened, they stepped out into a gym. The girl at the desk smiled at Sandy.

"Hi, Sandy, are you here for a workout?" she asked.

"No, Lena, I'm showing my girlfriend around the building," said Sandy with a smile as he drew Minnie close to his side. "Minnie, this is Lena. Lena, this is the love of my life, Minnie,"

"Hi, Minnie, welcome to Avorn gym. If you ever need a workout feel free to drop in. We can help you work out a fitness program just for you," said Lena.

"Thank you, I'll keep it in mind," said Minnie with a smile.

Sandy drew her on into the gym so she could get a look at everything. As soon as they made the rounds, he guided her back to the elevator, and with a smile and a wave at Lena, they entered the elevator to continue their tour.

They stopped, briefly on the fourth floor. Sandy pointed out the offices on the fourth floor. There were several lawyers and accountants. They didn't even get out of the elevator, but, continued down to the third floor to the Avorn Security offices.

Brenda looked up with a smile when they exited the elevator.

"Hi, Brenda, I'm showing Minnie around the building," said Sandy.

"You will love the boutique on the second floor," said Brenda. "They have some great outfits, and they are very reasonably priced," Brenda told Minnie with a smile.

"I can't wait to check it out," said Minnie smiling back at her.

Sandy led Minnie to the other elevator to go on down to the second floor. Brenda waved at them before the door closed. Sandy and Minnie waved back.

When they opened on the second floor, Sandy pointed out the boutique and the spa.

"Wow," said Minnie. "A spa right here in the building."

"Yeah," said Sandy grinning.

"Have you ever used it?" asked Minnie.

"Once, when I had a bad sprain, I used the hot tub and the steam room. It was great," said Sandy.

"I would love to see the steam room. Is it all male or can ladies use it, too?" asked Minnie.

They have a tag on the door. It can be switched between male and female, depending on who wants to use it," said Sandy.

Sandy guided her back to the elevator and down to the first floor.

"This floor has the restaurant. It also has a daycare, a barber shop and a beauty parlor. A lot of the employees in the building use the daycare. There is extra security to make sure the children are safe," said Sandy.

"I can see where having extra security would be a factor when working for a security firm," said Minnie.

They had seen a lot of security on their trip through the building.

The guards had either nodded or smiled at Sandy and continued on their way.

Would you like to stop for lunch?" asked Sandy.

"Sure," agreed Minnie.

"Hi, Lynn," greeted Sandy as they entered Andre's restaurant.

"Hello, Sandy, table for two?" asked Lynn.

"Yes, please," agreed Sandy.

Lynn guided them to a table and gave them menu's, to look at when they were seated.

"Wanda will be right with you," said Lynn. "Enjoy your lunch."

They were looking at the menu when Wanda arrived with glasses of water.

"What can I get for you?" asked Wanda.

Sandy glanced at Minnie. "I think I will have the lunch special," he said.

Minnie looked at the lunch special and felt her mouth water.

"That sounds good," she agreed.

"What would you like to drink?" asked Wanda.

"Iced sweet tea," said Minnie. Sandy nodded his agreement.

Wanda took their menus and left to get their orders.

Minnie looked around. "This place is amazing. How in the world did you and Sal end up working for Avorn Security?" she asked.

"We were hanging out in the gym, helping for free gym time. Alex was in there working out and he saw us sparing and asked if we would be interested in working for him. Of course, we jumped at the chance. We have never regretted it," said Sandy. "Alex is a great guy to work for."

Minnie nodded. "I can see he is," she agreed.

Wanda brought their food and they dug in. Minnie smiled at Sandy,

"You better enjoy this. I can't promise to provide such good food when we are together. I can cook, but not like this," said Minnie.

"I am not with you for your cooking. I love you. We will figure out everything else later," said Sandy.

Minnie looked at him and smiled through misty eyes.

"I love you, too. I have for years. I am so glad I don't have to hide it," she said.

"Me, too," agreed Sandy.

He reached across the table and squeezed her hand before continuing to eat.

Minnie and Sandy finished their meal and refused dessert when Minnie declared she couldn't eat another bite. Sandy paid the check and left a tip on the table before taking Minnie's hand and leading her back into the lobby. They entered the elevator, and Sandy pushed the button for the third floor.

"This is a great place," said Minnie. "You and Sal are very lucky to be working here."

"Yes, we are," agreed Sandy. "We don't usually spend so much time here in the building. We spend most of our time out doing our job."

"I really appreciate all of you helping me and rescuing Bobby," said Minnie.

Sandy squeezed her hand and kissed her forehead. "I love you, and Bobby is our best friend. There is no way we would leave you to fend for yourself."

"I love you, too. I just don't want to cause any problem with your job," said Minnie.

"If there was any problem, Alex would have let us know," said Sandy.

They left the elevator on the third floor and took the other elevator to the sixth floor. Brenda just smiled at them when they passed through. When they emerged on the sixth floor, they went to check on Bobby and see if any news had developed while they were gone.

Andrew glanced up at them from the sofa, as they entered. "Did you enjoy your tour?" he asked Minnie, smiling their way.

"Yes, I did. This is quite a place. I had no idea places like this were in our town," said Minnie.

"I don't think there are any others. I'm sure Avorn Security is unique," replied Andrew.

"It is certainly a beautiful place," she agreed.

Minnie smiled. "I think I will check on Bobby," she said.

Minnie left the room and Andrew looked at Sandy.

"Alex had me call Sal and Micky back. He wants to talk to all of us. He will be here soon."

"I wonder what is up," said Sandy.

Andrew shrugged. "I guess we will have to wait until Alex gets here to see," he said. Sandy nodded and took a seat to wait.

Minnie went to Bobby's bedside. He looked the same to her. She glanced at the nurse. "Has there been any response at all?" asked Minnie.

"No, the doctor came by and checked on him. He said everything was fine. Bobby needs to sleep as long as he can. All his vital signs are good. We just have to wait," replied the nurse.

Minnie sighed. "I know. I will try to be patient. He is looking better. Some of the bruising is fading."

"Yes, I have been rubbing a cream into his bruises. It will take some of the soreness out," said the nurse.

"Thank you," said Minnie smiling at the nurse.

"I will leave you to visit with your brother. While you are here, I'll take a short break. If you don't mind," said the nurse.

"That is fine. I'll be here," said Minnie.

"If there is any change, just call me," said the nurse.

Minnie nodded and went to take a seat beside Bobby's bed. She reached over and took Bobby's hand. His hand felt and looked better. The nurse must have been rubbing cream into his hand also, thought Minnie.

"Bobby, you are getting better. Soon, you will be awake and able to talk to us. I am almost afraid to hear what you have to say. I know it is going to make a huge difference in our lives. I hope this whole mess can be resolved without Mom getting hurt. She doesn't deserve to have to deal with Arnie and his friends.

How can he do this to her when she loves him so much?" Minnie sighed. "I guess there is no understanding some people. Mom loves him so much. I'm pretty sure he loves her, too. Maybe he is just weak. Maybe he got caught up in something he doesn't know how to get out of." Minnie shook her head and blinked her eyes.

"I don't know how to solve the problem. I just know I am not going back to live there while Arnie is there. I'm with Sandy now. He wouldn't want me living there. Mom wouldn't want me to move in with Sandy without marrying him first, but I don't know when Sandy wants to get married. I am still planning to take college classes. Maybe I can live on campus. I don't know if I can afford it. I have saved all of the money I can, but college is expensive. Maybe I can apply for financial aid."

Minnie stopped talking and gazed at the wall above Bobby's bed. She had been rambling on as she tried to think. She was trying to work things out in her head. Minnie shook her head and looked back down at Bobby. He looked so lost lying there so still and quiet.

"Is he going to be alright?" she asked her guardian angel.

"He's going to be fine. Don't worry. His guardian angel says to let him heal. If he wakes up now, we won't be able to stop him from going after the ones who did this to him. He needs to sleep while Alex works out the best way to handle everything."

Minnie nodded in agreement. She squeezed Bobby's hand again and then lay it back down by his side. She did not want to think about Bobby going after the ones who had done this to him. Minnie stood and walked over to the window. She looked out over the city. She looked around with awe. From this high up, she could see the whole city. It was hard to believe how anyone could live their life in such a building. Alex and Mariam were very lucky.

"I'm going to have to look out at night when it is all lit up. I bet it is really beautiful," murmured Minnie.

She stood looking around for a few minutes, until Lila returned. She smiled at Lila, before deciding to join Sandy and Andrew in the living room.

Sandy looked over at her and smiled when she entered the room. Minnie smiled back and joined him on the sofa.

Sandy put an arm around her and pulled her close to his side. "How is Bobby?" asked Sandy.

"He is doing good. I think the cream Lila is using on him is helping the bruises to heal. He is looking a lot better," said Minnie.

"Alex will be here soon. Sal and Micky will be joining us, too," said Andrew.

"Has something happened?" asked Minnie.

"Alex didn't say," said Andrew. "He just said he needed to talk to us."

There was a knock at the door.

Andrew went to open the door. Sal and Micky entered.

"Do you know what is going on?" Sal asked Andrew.

Andrew shook his head. "All I know is Alex wants to talk to all of us," replied Andrew.

Sal came over and leaning down kissed Minnie on the cheek.

"Everything is quiet on the home front," he said.

"I'm glad," responded Minnie with a smile and a sigh of relief.

"I think Arnie and his friends are staying low so they won't draw attention to themselves," said Micky.

They all turned and looked as Lila started through on her way to the kitchen. She took a bottle of water and started back to Bobby's room.

Micky's eyes lit up when he saw her.

"Hello," he said.

He went over closer to her and smiled in her eyes. "They would send me out on a job when there is such a lovely lady here," said Micky. "My name's Micky."

"Hello, Micky, my name is Lila," she replied.

"Beautiful name for a beautiful lady," said Micky taking her hand and squeezing it gently.

"It is nice to meet you," said Lila. She gently released her hand

and looked around to find the others watching with interested expressions on their faces. "I have to get back to my patient."

She smiled at them all then quickly hurried into Bobby's room and closed the door.

Sal shook his head. "Micky, Micky, you came on too strong. You will scare her off,"

Micky stood for a moment gazing after Lila, before turning back to the others.

"I have to make sure she remembers me. There is no telling where Alex is about to send us,"

"Is there any coffee made?" asked Sal heading for the kitchen.

"There should be plenty. I made a pot earlier," said Andrew as he sat watching the screens and keeping an eye on the building.

Micky followed Sal into the kitchen to fetch the coffee.

SEVEN

THEY HAD all settled down in the living room to enjoy their coffee and watch the news on TV when, after a knock at the door, Andrew opened the door for Alex to enter.

"Good, you are all here," said Alex looking around.

"Is Mariam coming?" asked Andrew still holding the door open.

"No," said Alex smiling. "She has story time at the day care."

"I bet the children love to be told stories," said Minnie.

"Yes," agreed Alex. "Mariam loves it, too. I think she misses teaching."

"I'm sure she would tell you if she wanted to teach," said Minnie. Alex smiled at Minnie and nodded.

Andrew closed the door and started back to his seat before stopping and looking at Alex. "Would you like coffee?" he asked.

"No, I'm fine," said Alex sitting in a chair facing everyone.

He waited for Andrew to take his seat before talking.

"The police chief wants to hire us to look into his police officer's murder," said Alex. "He thinks if someone outside of the police department investigates, there will be less chance people will claim cover up," said Alex.

"He could have a point," said Sal.

Alex nodded. "He could also be planning on making us be the fall guys when things don't turn out the way he wants them to."

"What did you tell him?" asked Micky.

"I told the two officers he sent to ask me, I would think about it and let him know," said Alex.

Alex looked around at each of them. "It might give us a chance to look around and find out what is going on without stirring up suspicion."

Sandy had been sitting quietly beside Minnie watching Alex.

"You want to take the case," said Sandy.

Alex smiled at Sandy and Minnie. "It would give us a good excuse to get Trey in to talk to Arnie's guardian angel without him knowing what is going on. Trey could find out if there is any chance of changing Arnie."

"Are Lori and the baby home, yet?" asked Andrew.

"They are going home tomorrow," said Alex. "Mariam could stay with Lori long enough for Trey to go with a couple of you to talk to Arnie."

"I'm in," said Sandy. "We need to know where we stand with Arnie. Minnie is going to have to be in contact with him as long as her mom is married to him. I don't want her in danger."

Alex nodded. "I understand. I felt the same way when Mariam was in danger."

"We are all in," said Sal. "Just tell us what you want us to do, and we will do our best to do it."

Micky and Andrew nodded their agreement.

Alex smiled at the group. "I'll let the chief know we are taking the case and ask him to send me all of the information he has. After I have studied his files and talked to the FBI agents I am in touch with, I will work up a plan and let you guys know what we are going to do. We won't do anything until Trey can join us tomorrow."

Alex rose and prepared to leave. "I'll let you know as soon as I have a plan. Thanks for everything."

The guys smiled and nodded to Alex as he left. Then, they turned and looked at each other.

"I don't know whether to hope for Trey to fix Arnie or for him to go to jail," said Sandy.

Sal and Micky laughed. "You will just have to wait and see what happens," said Sal.

"I know," said Sandy pulling Minnie close to his side. "I am not going to let him put you in danger," he promised Minnie.

"I need to talk to Mom," said Minnie. "Should I still tell her I am going out of town with my friends to check out colleges?"

Sal thought for a minute. "I think so. If thing change, you can always tell her you changed your mind and decided not to go."

Minnie nodded and rose to go to the kitchen to make her call.

Minnie punched in her mom's number and waited for her to answer.

"Hello," said Margo Croan.

"Hi, Mom," said Minnie.

"Hi, Minnie, are you on your way home?"

"Not yet, there has been a change of plans. Louanne and a couple of our friends are going to check out some colleges, to see which one they like the best. They asked me to go along with them. It will be a few days, but I am off work, so I thought I would go with them," said Minnie.

"That sounds like fun. It would help you to know more about the colleges, and, having your friends along will make you feel safer. I am glad you are pursuing your education," said Margo.

"Thanks, Mom. I love you," said Minnie.

"I love you, too. Call me each day so I will know you are alright," said Margo.

"I will," promised Minnie.

They hung up and Minnie stood for a minute, thinking. Sandy joined her and put an arm around her shoulder.

"Did you talk to your mom?" he asked.

"Yes," said Minnie. She turned her face up and looked at Sandy.

"I feel so guilty. Mom was so sweet to me. She only wants what is best for me, and I hate not being honest with her."

"I know," agreed Sandy. "I hate it, too. Hopefully, we can get everything straightened out and then you can be straight with her."

"I hope so," agreed Minnie. They turned and joined the others in the living room.

Sal and Micky were preparing to leave as Sandy and Minnie came back into the room.

"You guys heading out?" asked Sandy.

"Yeah," said Sal. "We have another case we need to finish up while we wait for Alex to tell us what to do about Arnie."

"You can call us if Alex needs us," said Micky.

"Okay," agreed Andrew.

When they were gone, Andrew turned to Sandy. "If you and Minnie are going to be here, I'll go over and keep an eye on Arnie and his friends. We don't need them to surprise us when we start investigating this case," said Andrew.

Sandy nodded. "Good idea; be careful and stay in touch. Don't take any chances."

"I won't," promised Andrew.

When he was gone, Minnie looked at Sandy and smiled. "Why do I get the feeling Andrew was getting tired of sitting around doing nothing?"

Sandy laughed. "I guess all of us are used to being busy. The only time we are sitting around is when we are on stakeout. Action goes with the job," said Sandy.

"Does that mean I am going to have to get used to you being in danger?"

"We are trained to take care of ourselves. Alex tries to minimize any danger. He tries to make sure we work in pairs so we have backup, and we only have to call, and he will send help at once. He really does look out for us. We also have our guardian angels. If they warn us not to do something, we don't do it. Alex drummed it into our heads to always listen and do as our guardian angels say," said Sandy.

Minnie put her arms around him and hugged him close. "I'm glad. The world would be a better place if everyone listened to their guardian angels," she said.

"Some people won't admit they exist," said Sandy.

Minnie shook her head. "It is so sad. They can be a great comfort to us."

Both of them sat up startled when they heard a noise coming from Bobby's room. They rose and hurried to the room. When they entered, they found Lila leaning over Bobby, holding his shoulder as he moaned and thrashed about.

"He's waking up," said Lila.

Sandy and Minnie went to the other side of the bed. Sandy held Bobby's other shoulder and started talking to him.

"You're safe, Bobby. Take it easy. We have you in a safe place. You don't have to worry about Arnie and his friends anymore. Just relax and let us take care of you," said Sandy.

Bobby settled down as if he was listening to Sandy's voice. His eyes had not opened, and after a minute or so, he seemed to fall back asleep.

"I don't think he was fully awake," said Lila.

"Does this mean he will be awake soon?" asked Minnie.

"It won't be much longer," agreed Lila. She drew back from the bed. "I need to call the doctor and let him know."

Lila took her phone from her pocket and went to the other room to call the doctor.

Sandy and Minnie stayed by Bobby's bed side. Minnie was holding his uninjured hand.

Sandy noticed the tears trembling on Minnie's lashes. She wiped them away, impatiently.

"This is good news," said Sandy. "Why are you crying?"

Minnie glanced up at him and then back at Bobby. "I am happy. These are happy tears," she said.

"How am I supposed to tell the difference?" asked Sandy looking at her and grinning. He was trying to distract her from worrying about Bobby.

"Maybe, because I am smiling through my tears," said Minnie. She looked at him and smiled again.

Sandy smiled back at her and leaning forward kissed her lightly.

"Now, I really am happy," said Minnie. Sandy started to kiss her again, but, was interrupted by Lila coming back into the room.

"The doctor will be by to check on Bobby as soon as he finishes his rounds at the clinic," said Lila.

She came over and checked Bobby's IV and his breathing. After checking, she went over and made some notations on the chart she had for Bobby.

"How is he doing?" asked Minnie.

"He is still sleeping, but it is not as deep a sleep as he has been in. He will probably be awake soon," said Lila. "Why don't you two go and watch TV? I'll call you if he wakes up. I don't want him to be disturbed by sensing someone with him."

"Minnie and Sandy stood from the bedside chairs and turned toward Lila.

"I didn't think about our presence bothering him," said Minnie. "I should have. I know it is hard to sleep with someone watching you."

She turned and took Sandy's hand and led the way into the living room. She led the way to the sofa and when Sandy sat down, Minnie sat as close to him as she could get without sitting in his lap.

Sandy put an arm around her and turned her so he could continue the kiss Lila had interrupted.

Minnie put her arms around him and returned his kiss. They were kissing passionately when the door opened, and Sal entered.

"Oops, sorry, didn't mean to interrupt," he said.

Sandy and Minnie had sat up and stopped kissing when Sal entered.

"Why are you here?" asked Sandy.

"I came to give you my notebook. It has all of my notes for the last few days and I thought Alex might ask for them.

He took a slim notebook out of his pocket and handed it to Sandy. As he handed the notebook to Sandy, he grinned at Minnie. "I want to let you know I'm really glad you are going to be my sister," said Sal.

Minnie smiled at him. "I'm glad to have another brother. At least, I'm glad to make it official. I have thought of you as my brother for years," said Minnie.

"Bobby's starting to wake up," said Sandy.

"Really, can he talk, yet?" asked Sal.

"No, but Lila has sent for the doctor. He was moving around before he settled down again," said Sandy.

Sal started for the door to Bobby's room.

"Lila asked not to disturb him before the doctor gets here to check him over," said Sandy.

Sal stopped and turned around.

"Oh, I guess I will see him when I get back. Micky is waiting for me downstairs," said Sal. "Call me if he wakes up."

"Okay," agreed Sandy as Sal let himself out the front door.

When he was gone, Sandy looked down at Minnie and smiled. "Now, where were we?" he asked.

"I think, just about here," said Minnie as she raised her lips and joined them with Sandy's.

"Yeah," murmured Sandy as he deepened the kiss.

They had just started kissing, when there was a knock at the door. Sandy sat up and scowled at the door. "I guess you had better see who it is," said Minnie with a smile."

"I guess so," said Sandy reluctantly rising and going to the door.

When he opened the door, Doctor Parks greeted him with a smile. "I understand my patient is waking," said Doctor Parks.

"He was stirring around a few minutes ago," said Sandy.

"I'll check him out and see what is going on," said Doctor Parks, heading for Bobby's room.

Sandy and Minnie waited in the living room as Doctor Parks was greeted by Lila in Bobby's room.

"Has there been any more movement?" he asked Lila.

"No, he has been still since the first movement," said Lila.

Dr. Parks took out his stethoscope and listened to Bobby's heartbeat. He then checked his chart and saw Bobby was doing just as he should.

"I don't think he is ready to wake up, yet. I think we have another 8 to 10 hours before we have any more movement from him," said Doctor Parks. "Just keep doing what you are doing and call me if there is any change."

"Yes, Doctor," agreed Lila.

Doctor Parks went out to the living room to talk to Sandy and Minnie.

They looked at him expectantly as he entered the room.

"He is fine, but I think it will be, at least 8 hours before he wakes up again. It is good he is starting to stir. When he started to wake up, the pain he was feeling probably shut him down for a little longer. When he wakes up again, he will probably stay awake, but he is going to be in pain. Lila has pain medicine for him, and she will keep a close watch on him and call me if there is any change," concluded Doctor Parks.

Minnie sat down with a sigh of relief and Sandy escorted the doctor to the door and thanked him for coming. Sandy turned and smiled at Minnie.

"It won't be long, now," he said with a smile.

"I can't wait for him to wake up, but I hate the idea of him in so much pain," said Minnie.

Sandy came over and taking Minnie's hand pulled her up into his arms.

"I am just grateful we found him in time." said Sandy.

"Me, too," agreed Minnie.

She gave Sandy a quick hug and pulled away.

"Why don't we try the television? Maybe there is some news on.

Besides, every time we start kissing someone interrupts," said Minnie glancing at Sandy with a grin.

Sandy laughed. "It does seem that way," he agreed.

Sandy took Minnie's hand and took her with him as he went over to the coffee table and found the remote. He found the right control for the TV and clicked it on.

Minnie sat down on the sofa and Sandy sat next to her and started changing the channels looking for a news station. When he found the news, he leaned back and prepared to watch.

Suddenly, Minnie sat forward with a gasp. They were watching the scene of an attempted carjacking. Minnie watched as her mom was being questioned by the police. While they watched Arnie hurried up and pulled her into a hug. Evidently, his fellow police officers had let him know what was going on, or Margo had called him. He looked like he was very worried about her.

EIGHT

SANDY TURNED the sound up so they could better hear what was being reported by the reporters, who were standing around the scene, trying to get a story.

"It seems as if the wife of a policeman was accosted as she left work for lunch," said the reporter. From what I understand, the carjacker approached the victim as she started to open her car door. She sprayed him with pepper spray and kneed him in the groin. When he was down on the ground moaning, she proceeded to call 911 and was sent help. The officers responded at once to the scene and now have the carjacker in custody on his way to get medical treatment."

The reporter smiled at the camera and raised a fist. "Score one for the good guys," she said.

She turned away and the camera man made another sweep of the scene before closing.

Minnie sat back with a sigh. "Mom looked okay," she said.

"She looked great," said Sandy. "I think she was very proud of how she handled herself. Your mom is one tough lady."

Minnie grinned. "Yes, she is," she agreed. "She loves Arnie so much. I hope we can fix it so she can stay with him," said Minnie.

"We will try, but it will be up to Trey and Arnie's guardian angel. If Trey can not get through to him, he won't be able to do anything for Arnie," said Sandy.

"I know," said Minnie. "I have no intention of living with Mom and Arnie again. As long as he isn't breaking the law, I will be hoping for the best for him and Mom."

Sandy pulled her close and grinned at her. "Do you suppose it is safe for us to kiss?" he asked with his lips close to hers.

"I'm willing to chance, it if you are," whispered Minnie.

Sandy's lips brushed hers lightly. He nibbled and scattered kisses around her face and then back on her lips.

Minnie moaned and started spreading kisses on his face, anywhere she could reach. Finally, their lips met in a deep and passionate kiss. When it was over, they were both breathing heavily. Minnie laid her head on Sandy's chest while she caught her breath.

"I love you," she whispered.

"I love you, too," said Sandy. "Will you marry me and make me the happiest man in the world?" asked Sandy.

"Yes, I will," said Minnie.

Sandy lowered his head for another kiss. They were both breathing hard when they came up for air again.

"When?" asked Sandy.

"When, what?" asked Minnie.

"When can we get married?" asked Sandy.

"When Bobby gets well enough to give me away," said Minnie.

Sandy pulled back and thought about it for a minute, then, he looked down at Minnie and smiled.

"Okay, my guardian angel said it wouldn't be long and for me to have patience and be happy I will soon be with my own true love," remarked Sandy.

"My guardian angel is pretty happy also. I can almost feel her doing a happy dance. I think they are very pleased with themselves," said Minnie, smiling at Sandy.

"I don't care. They can be pleased, and both do a happy dance as long as I get to end up with you as my wife," said Sandy.

Minnie raised her face for another kiss. Sandy was happy to oblige her. The TV played in the background forgotten and ignored by both of them.

"Where are we going to live?" asked Minnie after she could think again.

Sandy drew back and looked at her. "I don't know. I haven't thought about it," he said. "We could always start out in the apartment. I'm sure Sal wouldn't mind if we stay there while we are looking for a house."

"I think you need to talk with him before you decide about the apartment," said Minnie.

"I will," promised Sandy. "I make a good salary at Avorn. We can rent a house if you would rather have a house instead of an apartment."

"I don't mind an apartment at first. We won't need a house until we start a family," said Minnie. "I can start taking some of my college classes online. The ones I can't take online I can take at a local college so I can do day classes and be home at night."

"What are you going to be studying?" asked Sandy.

"I am going to be taking elementary education," said Minnie.

"You'll be a great teacher," said Sandy.

"I hope so. I love working with children. I have been saving money to pay my tuition and for my books," said Minnie.

Sandy kissed her and held her close.

"We will manage. As long as we are together, we can do anything. I want you to know I will do everything in my power to make your dreams come true. I want you to be happy," said Sandy.

"I will be happy as long as I'm with you, and I don't expect you to handle everything by yourself. I am going to be your partner. I will pull my weight. I never want to be a burden on you," said Minnie.

"You could never be a burden, and it will be a pleasure to be your partner in everything, even raising a family. Although you will have to carry the children, I will be right there with you all the way." Sandy kissed her again, and they both drew back from the kiss and smiled this promise into each other's eyes.

They settled into each other's arms and leaned back to watch TV. They still kissed often and really didn't get what was on TV. They were much more interested in real life in their arms.

While they were discussing their future, Andrew was following Arnie. He had just arrived at the Croan house when he saw Arnie hurry and take off in his car. Andrew followed him discretely. Arnie stopped at the local elementary school. Andrew watched as Arnie stopped his car and, leaving his door open, rushing over to where Minnie's mom stood talking to the police.

Arnie drew her into his arms and held her close. He looked like he was really worried about his wife.

Andrew did not know what was going on, but he continued to watch as an ambulance was loaded and driven away. The police smiled at Mrs. Croan and started to leave. Arnie held his wife close as he led her to his car and put her in the front seat.

Andrew followed Arnie's car to a restaurant, where Arnie and Mrs. Croan went inside and were shown to a table.

When lunch time was over Arnie took Mrs. Croan back to the school so she could complete her days work. It looked like he was trying to talk her into taking the rest of the day off, but she was shaking her head and after a goodbye kiss, she started for the inside of the school.

Arnie watched her enter the building before starting his car and leaving.

Andrew followed him as he made his way home.

As Arnie stopped at his house and started inside. Andrew passed on by without stopping. He made the block and came back around. He found a good place to park so he could keep a watch on the Croan house.

A short time later, one of Arnie's friends parked in his drive and went to the door. Arnie opened the door and let him inside.

"I sure wish I had a way to listen to what is being said in the house," said Andrew. "I know, I know," said Andrew to his guardian angel. "I won't do anything stupid. You don't have to worry. Alex would have my head if I messed up the investigation."

Andrew's guardian angel was very happy to be listened to. Most of the time, they were ignored. People did not believe in them, and when they didn't believe, they would not hear them speak.

Andrew noticed a man pass his car. He had a dog on a leash and was walking him. The man gave Andrew a curious look as he passed, so Andrew decided to leave. He didn't want to draw attention to himself. He started to go to Avorn Security, but decided to stop at a fast food place and get a burger before heading in.

After getting his food, Andrew called Sandy to see if there had been any news.

"Hello," said Sandy.

"Hi, I was checking to see if there was anything happening," said Andrew.

"We saw a news story about Minnie's mom getting car jacked," said Sandy.

"I wondered what was going on. I followed Arnie to the school. I could see something was going on, but I wasn't close enough to hear what was happening," said Andrew.

"Are you still watching Arnie?" asked Sandy.

"No, he is at home with a friend, but a dog walker was getting curious, so I left," said Andrew.

"Are you on your way back here?" asked Sandy.

"I stopped for a burger, but I will come in then," said Andrew.

"After you finish eating, why don't you do a quick drive by and see if there is anything new going on with Arnie before you come in," suggested Sandy.

"Okay, I'll see you in about an hour," agreed Andrew.

"Is everything okay with Andrew?" asked Minnie when Sandy hung up the phone.

"Yes, he followed Arnie to the school and back home and decided to leave when a dog walker became curious," replied Sandy.

"Why did you want him to drive by the house again?" asked Minnie.

"I don't know. It was just a feeling I had. It may mean nothing, but I thought it wouldn't hurt for Andrew to check it out," said Sandy with a shrug.

Minnie smiled at him. "We should always listen to our feelings. Mom used to tell me, if it doesn't feel right, go another direction. She said feelings were sometimes our guardian angel's way of letting us know something is wrong or needs changing," said Minnie.

"Yeah," said Sandy grinning. "Mom used to say the same thing to us when we were small."

"I guess it is a mom thing. They didn't want to try to explain our guardian angels to us before we could understand," said Minnie.

"I think they didn't want us to talk about our guardian angels. They were afraid we would become targets for bullies and witch hunters," said Sandy.

Minnie nodded her head. "They were trying to keep us safe."

"Are you hungry? I can make us a sandwich. I wonder if Lila would like a sandwich," said Sandy.

Minnie laughed. "I would love a sandwich. I will ask Lila if she would like one."

She gave Sandy a quick kiss and headed for the bedroom before he could deepen the kiss. Sandy smiled and headed for the kitchen.

"Hi, Lila," said Minnie quietly as she entered the bedroom. "Sandy is making some sandwiches and we wondered if you would like one."

"Yes, I am beginning to get a little hungry," said Lila smiling.

Minnie glanced at Bobby. "Has there been any more movement?" she asked.

Lila shook her head. "No, he is resting quietly. There has been no change."

Minnie frowned as she looked Bobby over again. He looked so peaceful. She was anxious to see him awake, but she was going to have to take a page out of Sandy's book and be patient.

Minnie looked over and smiled at Lila and they both turned and headed for the kitchen.

Sandy had sandwich makings spread out on the counter. He had the bread and condiments sitting out as well. He was filling glasses with iced tea.

"I thought I would let you fix your own sandwiches so you could put what you like on them," said Sandy as he took the glasses and put them where they would be close to them, but not get in the way.

"This looks great," said Minnie as she started making her sandwich.

"Yes, it does," agreed Lila as she followed Minnie's example and started on a sandwich.

Sandy followed the girl's example and started his own sandwich.

Minnie looked at Sandy and grinned. "It's a shame we don't have any of your mom's chocolate cake, for desert," she said.

"Yeah, I am going to have to drop by and see if Mom has any cake left," agreed Sandy.

Lila looked at them and smiled. "You sound like you miss your mom's cooking," she said.

"Sometimes," agreed Sandy. "We visit her often. Sal and I really enjoy having our own place, but Mom and Dad will always be home."

"I know what you mean. I couldn't wait to be own my own and not have to answer to anyone but myself, but it is always nice to visit home and spend time with my mom and dad. When we get together with my sisters and their families, it is really nice," agreed Lila.

Minnie had been sitting quietly listening to Lila and Sandy talk. She did not have the same feeling of home they had. She missed her mom, but Bobby, Sal and Sandy had always meant home to her. Mostly Sandy, she couldn't remember a time when she had not felt

Sandy belonged with her. He was her home. When he was with her, she was okay. She knew he would keep her safe.

"He is your heart's true love," said her guardian angel.

"I know," agreed Minnie with satisfaction.

Minnie smiled at Sandy and started putting away the sandwich makings left after their sandwiches were made.

Lila started to help, but Minnie shook her head and told her she had it, so Lila went back to check on Bobby and Minnie finished cleaning the kitchen. Sandy went to check the news to see if anything else was happening.

When Minnie joined Sandy in the living room, she found him shifting through the security cameras, checking out the building.

"Is anything wrong?" asked Minnie.

"No," said Sandy reaching out an arm and pulling Minnie close to his side. "Everything looks calm. It makes me nervous. I keep thinking it is the calm before the storm."

Minnie shivered. She watched as Sandy looked from floor to floor. She did not know what Sandy was looking for, but she trusted his instincts.

Sandy held her close for comfort and kept switching pictures on the surveillance cameras. He went from floor to floor. He watched the security guards go up and down the halls. Brenda was at her desk on the third floor. She was working and looked fine. Frank was sitting at his desk on the first floor. He was watching to make sure no one entered the building who was not supposed to be there. He looked calm. Everything looked quiet and peaceful. He just couldn't shake the feeling he was missing something. Sandy sighed and looked through the floors one more time. Nothing seemed to be wrong.

"What am I missing," he asked his guardian angel.

"I don't sense anything wrong," replied his guardian angel.

"Well, keep alert and let me know if anything changes," said Sandy.

"Okay," agreed his guardian angel.

Sandy laid the remote down and turned away from the monitors.

NINE

MINNIE GRINNED as she looked up into Sandy's face. Sandy, feeling her gaze glanced down at her.

"Have I got something on my face?" he asked.

Minnie smiled. "No, I was just thinking how much I love having you close."

Sandy gave her a squeeze. "I can't seem to get enough of touching you. It's as if I can't touch you, I'll find out this is all a dream and I will be back to wanting you, but not knowing if you want me."

Minnie snuggled closer to him. "I know what you mean. I have a hard time believing it really is happening. I have been waiting for you to notice me for so long, I had almost given up hope," she whispered.

"I noticed you, I was just waiting for you to be old enough to keep Bobby and Sal from beating the crap out of me for lusting after their little sister," said Sandy.

Minnie laughed. "They would have had to go through me to get to you," she said.

"My hero," said Sandy giving her a kiss on the forehead.

"You better believe it," agreed Minnie. "Just as you are my hero, we belong together. I refuse to let anyone stand between us, now that I know you love me."

"No one would dare," agreed Sandy smiling at her determined face.

Minnie looked at the monitors Sandy had been studying.

"What is happening?" she asked.

Sandy looked back at the monitors, thoughtfully. "Do you suppose we could go through the tunnel and plant a listening device in your room, so we could hear what is being said?" asked Sandy.

Minnie shook her head. "The tunnel is very small. I could barely get through. It's not big enough for any of you, except maybe Andrew."

"I don't want to take a chance on Arnie and his friends finding the tunnel," said Sandy.

Minnie smiled. "They won't find it. I turned the lock before I started down the stairs. They will not accidentally open it from above.'

"Good," said Sandy. "We will have to open it if we want to enter through there anytime."

"Why would you need to go out through the tunnel?" asked Minnie.

"We wouldn't, but you might need it if you plan on going there anytime before we are married. Your mom is going to think it is strange if you never go there," said Sandy.

Minnie sighed. "I know, I have been thinking about that. I was hoping Trey could have a shot at Arnie before I have to return."

"Maybe he will," agreed Sandy. "Alex is working on it. We will just have to hope Trey can get through to Arnie."

"I'll keep my fingers crossed," said Minnie holding up two hands with crossed fingers on each.

Sandy laughed and kissed her on the tip of her nose.

Minnie looked thoughtful, then, she smiled.

"What is it?" asked Sandy.

"My guardian angel told me to have a little faith. She said everything is going to work out in the end," said Minnie.

Sandy smiled. "I'm not worried about the end. The end is going to be with me. I just don't want anything to happen to you before we can be together."

"I have never felt safer in my life than I do now in your arms," said Minnie.

Sandy kissed her and held her close.

Sandy glanced at the monitor and sighed. "The doctor is here," he remarked as he went to open the door for Dr. Parks.

"Hello, Dr. Parks," said Sandy.

"Hello, Sandy, Miss Kelp," said Dr. Parks.

"Hello, Dr. Parks, please call me Minnie," Minnie replied with a smile.

"Minnie," agreed Dr. Parks. "Has your brother tried to wake up again?" he asked.

"Not since your last visit," said Minnie.

Dr. Parks nodded. "It sometimes takes several tries before a patient fully awakens. Let me see how he is doing."

Dr. Parks headed for Bobby's room and Minnie and Sandy followed him in.

After greeting Lila, Dr. Parks went straight to Bobby's bedside. He read his chart and checked him out.

Dr Parks turned and faced Minnie and Sandy. "He is doing fine. Lila has been taking good care of him. He is getting closer to the surface. We just have to be patient. I know how hard it can be to be patient, but this sleep is the best thing for Bobby right now. It is giving him a chance to heal without putting any strain on his body. You know, if Bobby was awake, he would be trying to do too much. He would not relax and let his body heal. This sleep is his body's way of giving him a chance to heal. His guardian angel is also helping to keep him asleep."

Dr. Parks smiled. "Earlier when Bobby started waking up, his guardian angel knew he wasn't ready, so he helped Bobby go back to sleep for a while," said Dr, Parks.

"Wow!" exclaimed Minnie. "I didn't know they could do that."

"Our guardian angels can do a lot more than anyone knows. We just have to give them a chance," said Dr. Parks.

Lila smilingly agreed with the doctor.

Sandy and Minnie stepped back, and left Dr. Parks talk to Lila about Bobby's care.

When he finished talking to Lila, Sandy and Minnie accompanied him back to the front room, where He prepared to leave.

They heard a gasp and a cry from Bobby's room and all three of them turned and hurried back to the room.

They found Lila trying to hold Bobby back as he tried to get out of bed.

Dr, Parks and Sandy hurried to help Lila.

Minnie stood at the foot of the bed and looked at Bobby. "That's enough, Bobby," she said loudly. "Stop this at once, and, behave yourself."

Bobby stopped struggling and listened. Minnie's voice got through to him. He lay back and opened his eyes. He looked straight at Minnie.

"Minnie, what are you doing here?" he asked hoarsely.

"I'm trying to stop you from giving the doctor and nurse a hard time," said Minnie.

Bobby looked around with his eyes. He did not move his head. "Where am I? How did I get here?" asked Bobby. He could barely make himself understood, his voice was so scratchy.

Lila went to the head of his bed and offered him a drink of water through a straw.

Bobby accepted a few sips of water before turning away from it. He looked back at Minnie.

"You are at the Avorn Security building. Sal and Sandy rescued you and brought you here," said Minnie.

Bobby glanced at Sandy, who had moved to stand beside Minnie. "Thanks," said Bobby. "How did you know I needed rescuing?"

"Minnie told us," said Sandy. "She was worried about you."

"I know you all have a lot of questions," said Dr. Parks. "Bobby needs to rest his voice before he does any more explaining."

"Okay," agreed Minnie. "We'll be in the other room. If you need anything just tell Lila. She will let us know." Minnie started to turn and leave, but, looked back at Bobby. "I love you, big brother. I'm glad we found you before it was too late."

Tears started in her eyes and Sandy put an arm around her and she leaned close to him as they left the room.

Bobby watched them go and wondered at how Sandy was so protective of Minnie. Bobby looked up at the nurse and tried to smile, but it was more of a grimace. He closed his eyes and fell back to sleep.

Dr. Parks followed Minnie and Sandy into the front room.

Minnie looked up at him through misty eyes. "Is he okay?" she asked.

"He is fine. He has fallen back to sleep. He will be better each time he wakes up," said Dr. Parks.

"Why was he fighting everyone when he woke up?" asked Minnie.

"He probably thought he was still in the abandoned factory," said Sandy.

Dr. Parks nodded his agreement. "It was a natural reaction. It was the last memory he had before he lost consciousnesses, He thought he was still fighting his kidnappers," said Dr. Parks.

Minnie shivered.

"I need to go. I have patients to see to," said Dr. Parks.

"Thanks for coming," said Sandy as he went to open the door for him.

"Yes, thanks for all of your help," said Minnie.

"Just doing my job," said Dr. Parks with a smile as he left.

Sandy closed the door after him and came back to Minnie and put his arms around her and held her close.

"I'm beginning to think Bobby might be okay," said Minnie.

Sandy looked down at her curiously. "Were you in doubt?" he asked.

"He looked so beat up and he was unconscious so long," said Minnie with a sigh. "I didn't know what to think."

Sandy nodded. "I know, it was hard seeing him like that, but he is getting better. If we can keep him from getting into any more situations like this again, we may be able to keep him alive."

"Mom is going to be very upset with me if she finds out I have been keeping Bobby's condition from her all of this time," said Minnie.

"I'm sorry, but there is no way we can let her know until we take care of Arnie," said Sandy.

"I know," agreed Minnie. "I won't say anything."

They both turned and looked at the door as it opened, and Sal and Micky entered followed by Andrew. Sal looked at Sandy with eyebrows raised questionably when he saw Minnie's wet eyes.

"Bobby woke up for a couple of minutes, but he is sleeping again, now," said Sandy.

"Did he say anything?" asked Micky.

"Not really, he was disoriented. Dr. Parks was here. He checked him over and said he would get more lucid each time he woke up," said Sandy.

Sal nodded. Have you heard anything else from Alex?" he asked.

Sandy shook his head. "No, not yet," he said. Andrew went over and started looking at the monitors.

"I thought you were keeping an eye on Arnie," said Sandy.

"I was," agreed Andrew. "Some of the people in the neighborhood were starting to notice me, so I decided to leave for a while."

Sandy nodded. "We don't want to have anyone warning Arnie he is being watched," agreed Sandy.

Sandy looked at Micky. Sal had headed for the kitchen. Sandy shook his head and grinned. His little brother was always hungry.

"Did you and Sal wrap up your cases?" he asked Micky.

"Yes," said Micky. "We finished our reports and e-mailed them to Alex."

"What were you two working on?" asked Andrew.

"Mrs. Malino asked us to locate her missing son," said Micky.

"Did you find him?" asked Andrew.

"Yes," nodded Micky. "He was hanging out with some friends. They were smoking weed and lounging around, taking advantage of the boy's home, while his parents were gone to check on a sick relative. The parents arrived home just after we located him and they were furious. They kicked everyone out and grounded the boy, taking his phone and computer. We took young Malino home to his mom."

Micky laughed. "After she finished hugging him and checking to be sure he was alright, she grounded him and took his phone, car keys and computer and informed him he was working in her flower shop until he paid her back for the cost of finding him."

"I don't think he will try anything like this again anytime soon," said Micky.

"There were a bunch of boys who got a wake up call, along with their parents," said Sal joining them with a sandwich in his hand.

"The parents of the boy, who was throwing the party, called the parents of all of the boys, who were there when they returned. They told them all what the boys had been doing. Most of the parents appreciated the calls and thanked them for calling. They promised to handle their boy's punishment. A few couldn't be bothered and fused at the parents for leaving the boys unsupervised," said Micky.

Sandy shook his head. "Those boys need help now before they get into things they can't get out of."

"Some people have to learn the hard way," said Micky.

They all nodded agreement, saddened by the thought of the boys' future without being taught the right way to live.

"Has there been any word from Alex?" asked Sal taking a seat on the sofa and watching Andrew change from one monitor to another as he scanned the building.

"No," said Sandy. He guided Minnie over to a large recliner and pulled Minnie down into his lap as he sat down.

Minnie leaned back and relaxed in his arms as she listened to the conversation between the guys.

Sal grinned at her and went back to watching the monitors.

Andrew had his attention fixed on the monitor for the first floor. He was staring at it fixedly.

"What's going on?" asked Micky going closer to see what Andrew was looking at.

Andrew quickly changed floors. "Nothing," said Andrew.

Micky grinned. "You were watching Wanda, again," said Micky. "Why don't you ask her out?"

Andrew shook his head. "She doesn't even know who I am. She wouldn't go out with me."

He looked so dejected; Minnie felt sorry for him.

"Why don't you go down to the restaurant to eat? If she sees you around enough, she will become more familiar with you and then you can ask her out," she suggested.

Andrew looked over at her briefly and gave her a sad smile. "I have been down there a few times, with Sal and Micky. She only watched them. I don't think she even noticed I was there."

Minnie shook her head, "You have to go by yourself. Talk nice to her and let her get to know you with no distractions. It wouldn't hurt if you left her a big tip."

Sandy, Sal, and Micky laughed at this last remark.

"Waitresses always remember when they receive a large tip," agreed Sal. "I have used that tactic a few times."

"Did it work?" asked Andrew.

"Sometimes," said Sal with a shrug.

"It can't hurt to try," said Minnie.

Andrew didn't say anything else, but he looked thoughtful.

Lila came into the room. After a shy glance at Sal, she started toward the kitchen. Sal rose and followed her out.

Minnie glanced at Sandy and grinned. He had been watching

Sal's reaction, also. He didn't say anything, just smiled and kissed her gently.

Micky and Andrew were still watching the monitors. They were discussing the people, who were traversing the halls of Avorn Security. Micky smiled as they focused on the fifth floor and the gym.

"There is Charlie and Moss. They are headed in for a workout," said Micky.

"Are they friends of yours?" asked Minnie.

Micky looked at her. "More like sparing partners," said Micky.

Micky was still smiling. He looked like he was imagining getting into the ring with one or both the men.

She looked at Sandy. "Have you sparred with them?" she asked.

"A time or two, mostly Sal and I sparred each other," said Sandy.

"I'm going to have to watch you two spar sometime," she said.

"I would like for you to be there cheering me on," agreed Sandy.

Minnie smiled at him and raised her mouth for a kiss.

TEN

"ALEX IS HERE," said Andrew leaving the monitors to open the door.

Alex greeted them all as he came in the door. He had papers in his hand and held them up to show the men.

"I have the report from the police department. It includes police statements and an autopsy report on the policeman who was shot," said Alex.

Lila and Sal entered from the kitchen. Lila smiled, and spoke to Alex, but continued into Bobby's room. Sal joined the others to see what the police report said.

Minnie had moved to a seat on the sofa, when Alex entered, and Sandy joined the others looking at the reports.

All at once Sandy looked up and was still for a minute. He then turned toward the monitors and started changing to different floors. The others stopped and looked at him curiously.

Sandy stopped and cursed. He quickly punched the button for Frank at the front desk.

"Frank, we have two men with guns in the elevator from the

garage to the first floor. You need to stop the elevator and put them to sleep," said Sandy.

The others crowded around the monitor to watch. Minnie stared at them in amazement.

The men heaved a sigh of relief as they watched the men sink to the floor of the elevator after breathing in the sleeping gas.

Alex punched the button to Frank again. "Good work, Frank, have some security guards suit up in gas masks and take those two into custody after taking their guns. Have them brought to the conference room on the third floor," said Alex.

They watched the security men, in gas masks, take the men from the elevator after taking their weapons.

Alex looked at Sandy. "How did you know they were there?" he asked. "I have been having a feeling something was about to happen and I asked my guardian angel to keep an eye open for trouble. When he spotted the men with guns, he alerted me to look for them," said Sandy.

Alex grinned and patted Sandy on his back. "Thanks, thank your guardian angel, too. Now, let's go down and see what these men have to say for themselves," said Alex turning to the door with all of the guys following him.

Sandy came over to Minnie, where she was standing watching what was going on. He leaned down and kissed her gently.

"You stay here with Lila. I'll be back as soon as I find out what those two were up to," he said.

Minnie just smiled and nodded. Sandy gave her shoulders a squeeze and followed the others out the door. He caught up with them at the elevator to the third floor. They all crowded into the elevator. It seemed very full, with so many large men in it at once.

When they exited the elevator on the third floor, Brenda looked at them curiously. She had already seen the security guards carry the two men to the conference room. Alex nodded to her, but, didn't stop to talk. He and the others continued past her to the conference room.

The two men were there handcuffed to chairs. They were just starting to wake up.

One of the men groaned and opened his eyes. He looked at Alex in surprise. His eyes widened as he looked at the others and realized he was handcuffed to his chair.

"What's going on?" he asked.

"That is my question," said Alex. "Why were you entering my building carrying guns?"

The man looked at his partner as he started groaning and moving.

"What did you do to us?" he asked.

"You have been given a harmless sleeping gas," said Alex. "You didn't answer my question."

"We were here to pick up Andy's kid. He is in daycare here," he answered.

"Did you need to have assault rifles to pick up the child?" asked Alex.

The guy looked around at the other men and squirmed. "We were on our way to the practice range and we didn't want to leave them in the car while we picked up the kid," he said.

"I see," said Alex. "What's the child's name and age?" asked Alex.

"Amory Hanks, he is four years old," said the man.

"What are you and your friend's names?" asked Alex.

He was writing down the names.

"I'm Jessie Dills and he is Andy Hanks."

Alex took the information and his phone and went into the hall. He called the daycare and confirmed the child was there. He asked if the father had permission to pick up the child. The attendant looked up the child's record and said, no.

"The only person listed to pick up the child is his Aunt Sally Swills," she replied.

"I see," said Alex. He hung up and called Trey.

"Hello," answered Trey.

"Hi, Trey, I was wondering if you could get away for a while. I have a situation here at the security building. I could really use your help," said Alex.

"Sure, let me tell Lori where I am going and I'll be right there," said Trey.

"Is Stan still keeping an eye on her and the baby?" asked Alex.

"Yeah, He is here. They will be fine," replied Trey.

"Okay, I'll see you, soon," said Alex hanging up the phone.

He turned and went back into the conference room.

Everyone turned and looked at Alex as he entered. He didn't say anything, just went around the table and sat down across from the two men.

Sandy and Andrew went around and took seats on the other side of the table, down from Alex. Sal and Micky were leaning against the wall, watching the men handcuffed to the chairs.

Andy had fully awakened and was furious.

"You have no right to treat us like this," he stated.

"You came into my building carrying assault weapons. I have the right to protect the people in this building," said Alex. "Would you rather I call the police?"

Alex saw the leap of fear in the men's eyes before they both shook their heads.

"There's no need for the police," said Jessie. "We don't want to cause no trouble," he said.

Andy looked at him like he didn't agree with the statement. He looked like he would love to cause all kinds of trouble, thought Alex.

"Why were you here to pick up your son?" asked Alex.

"Because Sally wouldn't let me see him, I just wanted to spend some time with my kid," said Andy.

"Where does his aunt work?" asked Alex.

"She works in the beauty parlor on first floor," said Andy.

"Where is the child's mother?" asked Alex.

"She had an accident. She is dead," said Andy.

"How did the aunt end up with the child?" asked Alex.

"The judge listened to the lies about me and he gave her custody. I only get supervised visitation once a month," said Andy.

The door opened and Trey entered. He received smiles and greetings from the guys and joined Alex at the table. He sat down beside Andy.

"Have we started handcuffing our guests?" he asked.

Alex smiled. "Thanks for coming. Andy and Jessie entered the building carrying assault weapons and were going to try to take Andy's son from daycare without permission," explained Alex.

"I see," said Trey. He leaned back in his chair and closed his eyes. He didn't say anything for a few minutes, and everyone stayed quiet. The men in handcuffs began to shift uncomfortably.

Trey opened his eyes and looked at Andy. "I can help you with your anger if you will let me," he said.

Andy sat staring at him. He didn't say anything for a minute, then, he shook his head. "I didn't mean to hurt her. It was an accident. I just didn't want her to leave me. I loved her and my son. I didn't want her to leave." Andy broke down and started crying.

Trey put his hand on Andy arm and concentrated while Andy cried. He didn't try to stop him from crying. He was talking to Andy's guardian angel.

"You don't want to hurt anyone. You love your son. You are going to control your anger and work to prove you are worthy to be in your son's life. You are not going to show anything but love to your son and his Aunt. When you leave here you will take your friend and go back to work. Tell everyone how sorry you are to have caused a problem and promise to not let it happen again. Thank Mr. Avorn for letting you visit his building before you leave."

Trey removed his hand from Andy and went around to his friend Jessie. He put his hand on Jessie's arm and closed his eyes.

"You are going to calm your friend down. Encourage him to have patience and work to regain his son's love and trust. At no time are you going to encourage him to go against the boy's aunt or the law. You are going to be a good friend to him. You are both going to forget about the purpose of this trip today. You were only curious to see the building where the boy and his aunt spent so much time. You will not remember being handcuffed or put to sleep. Thank Mr. Avorn for letting you visit and go back to work."

Trey looked at Alex and Alex handed him the key to the handcuffs. Trey unlocked Jessie and then went around and unlocked Andy.

Alex smiled. "Thanks for coming," he said to Trey.

"No problem," assured Trey.

Sal would you and Micky show Mr. Hanks and Mr. Dills the way to the garage?" asked Alex.

"Sure, Boss," said Micky.

Andy and Jessie rose from their chairs and faced Alex. "Thanks for letting us see the building," said Andy. "I hope we didn't cause any trouble."

"No trouble at all. It always nice to see friendly neighbors," assured Alex. He came around and shook both men's hands before sending them off with Sal and Micky.

After the men left, Andrew looked at Alex. "Are you going to give them back their guns?" he asked.

"No, I think I will hang onto them. I see no reason to tempt fate," said Alex.

They all stood and left the conference room. Trey went with them. They headed back to the sixth floor to continue their look at the police department case.

When Sal and Micky reached the first floor with Andy and Jessie, they met Sally Swills in the hall getting out of the elevator from the garage.

She looked in surprise and suspicion at Andy and Jessie.

"Andy, Jessie, what are you doing here?" she asked.

"I just wanted to see where my son spent his days," said Andy.

"Have you been to the daycare?" asked Sally.

"No," said Andy shaking his head. "Mr. Avorn was showing me some of the building."

Sally's eyes widened. "You met Alex Avorn?"

"Yes, he was very nice to us," said Andy. "We have to go back to work, now. Tell Amory I love him, and I'll see him soon."

Sally stared at him. She couldn't believe how pleasant he sounded. She nodded as Sal and Micky escorted the men into the elevator and pushed the button for the garage.

Sally was still standing in the hall by the elevator when Sal and Micky returned.

She looked at Micky. "Was Andy telling the truth? Did he really meet Alex Avorn?" she asked.

Micky nodded. "Yes, he did." Micky looked at her as if he wanted to say something and then shook his head as if changing his mind.

"What is it?" asked Sally.

"I was just wondering how his wife died. He seemed all broken up about it," said Micky.

Sally took a deep breath. "My sister's death was an accident. The neighbors told the police about Shelia and Andy fighting. They thought Andy may have pushed her. He didn't push her. Andy wouldn't hurt anyone. Shelia slipped on some ice and hit her head on a step. She was taking her things to her car so she could leave Andy. He was begging her to stay when she slipped."

"Why did the judge give you custody of the boy?" asked Sal.

"Because of the neighbors telling him Shelia was pushed. I agreed to take Amory to keep the judge from putting him in foster care. I'm trying to give things time to settle down before trying to get the judge to give Amory back to his dad," said Sally. "The accident wasn't his fault. He doesn't deserve to lose his son."

"Why was your sister leaving him?" asked Sal.

"She had a boyfriend. Before you jump to conclusions, Andy didn't know, and I am not going to tell him. He has enough to deal with," said Sally.

Sal nodded. "We won't say anything. Who was the judge on the case? Alex knows a lot of people, maybe he can help," said Micky.

"It was Judge Barbara Leeks," said Sally. "Tell Mr. Avorn I appreciate anything he can do to help. I really want to get Amory and Andy back together."

"I don't know if he can help, but it won't hurt to try," said Micky.

Sally nodded. "I know. I have to get back to work," said Sally looking at her watch.

"We will let you know if we find out anything," said Micky.

"Thanks," said Sally starting for the beauty parlor.

Sal and Micky took the elevator to the third floor where they were greeted by a curious Brenda. They waved hello and continued to the elevator to the sixth floor where they joined Alex and the rest of the group discussing the case from the police station. They told Alex about seeing Sally and how she was sure her sister's death was an accident. They gave him the judge's name to look into the case.

"I can tell you, now. Andy's wife's death was an accident. His guardian angel told me he tried to catch her when he saw she was falling. That is why the neighbors thought he pushed her. He loved her. He only wanted her to stay. He didn't hurt her," said Trey.

"It looks like I will be getting in touch with the judge," said Alex with a grin.

Alex looked at the name of the judge and smiled. "This may be easier than we thought," he said.

"Do you know her?" asked Trey.

"Yes, we went to school together and we have helped each other out a few times," said Alex. He took out his phone and placed a call to Judge Leeks' office.

"Hello, I would like to speak to Judge Leeks. Would you tell her Alex Avorn is calling?"

"Hello, Alex, how are you today? I haven't talked to you in a while. Congratulations on your marriage," said Judge Leeks.

"Thank you, Barbara. I'm doing fine. How is the judge business going? You still loving it?" asked Alex.

Barbara laughed. "Always," she said. "What can I do for you today?"

"I'm calling about a case of yours. It's the Hanks case, where the wife died in an accident, and you awarded custody of the four-year-old boy to his aunt," said Alex.

"I remember the case. Why are you calling about this case? It was suggested the father may have helped his wife have her accident. There was not sufficient evidence to charge him, but I wasn't going to leave the boy in danger," said the Judge.

"It was an accident. I have it on good authority that the father loved his wife and son and would never hurt them. He was trying to catch her when she fell," said Alex.

"On what authority?" asked the Judge.

"His guardian angel said it. I had Trey do a check for me. His guardian angel was clear it was an accident," said Alex.

The judge sighed. "If he ever gets tired of the security business you can send Trey to me. He would be a big help around here," she said.

"I'll be sure and tell him. It was nice talking to you, Barbara," said Alex.

"Thanks for your help. I will get the Hanks case straightened out," said the judge.

They hung up and Alex turned to Trey.

Judge Leeks wanted me to tell you if you get tired of working for me, she has a job for you," said Alex with a smile.

"I don't think so," said Trey. Lori and I like working for Avorn Security. She may decide to leave me if I take away her favorite pastime," said Trey with a grin.

They turned back to the case they were discussing.

ELEVEN

THEY CARRIED the papers to the dining room table and spread the out so they could all study them. Sal and Micky paid close attention to the crime scene photos. They wanted to see if the scene was the same as when they left there with Bobby.

"The chair he is tied to, has been turned facing the door," said Micky.

"Yeah, it was turned with him facing the inside when we left him," said Sal.

"I guess, whoever shot him turned him and tried to question him," said Andrew looking at the photo.

"It's possible he could have scooted the chair around trying to get free," said Alex.

"The chair was heavy. I don't think he could have moved it without help," said Sal.

"It says here that there were powder burns on his forehead," said Alex studying the autopsy report.

"The gun must have been held against his head when it was fired," said Trey.

"It does sound like a hit," said Sandy.

"Maybe," said Alex. "It could have been one of his friends mad because he had lost Bobby. They sound like they were all pretty drunk according to what you all reported."

"Yeah, they were. They may have held the gun so close so they could be sure not to miss," said Micky.

The guys shook their heads. It was hard to imagine how anyone could do this to a friend.

Trey looked up from the report. "It says the policeman was working undercover. Do we know if it is true?" he asked.

Alex shook his head. "We don't know if we can believe anything said by the police department. They may be trying to cover for their guy."

"Why would they bring you into it if they want a cover up?" asked Trey.

"I don't know. Maybe the chief has his suspicions about some of the guys and doesn't know who he can trust," said Alex. "He may also be trying to take the heat off the department."

"Didn't you say Minnie and Bobby's stepdad is involved with the slain policeman?" asked Trey.

"Yes, they were drinking buddies," said Sal.

Trey nodded. "I need to go and meet him and see what his guardian angel has to say," said Trey.

"You want to go over now?" asked Alex.

"Yes, just a short visit, we can ask a few questions and I can talk to his guardian angel. We can let him know we may be back later with more questions," said Trey.

"Okay," agreed Alex. "I'll go with you, and Micky can go with us."

He shook his head as Sal started to say something. "I don't want you or Sandy there. You are neighbors and I don't want to draw his attention to the building while Bobby is here," said Alex.

"Mrs. Croan will be home from work by now," said Sandy.

"We are not going to upset anyone," said Alex. "We have the

chief's okay to talk to any of his officers. If Trey finds out anything we can go back sometime when Mrs. Croan is at work."

"We don't want to make him suspicious," said Alex. "I also want to put a listening device there somewhere so we can listen to the friends when they get together tomorrow."

Andrew grinned. "I was just thinking about that while I was watching him today."

Alex grinned. "We'll stop by the penthouse so I can let Mariam know where I am going and pick up a listening device," said Alex.

Alex headed for the door and Trey and Micky followed.

"Micky, why don't you go and get the car?" suggested Alex. "Trey and I will by right with you."

Micky nodded and headed for the elevator to the third floor. Alex and Trey took the stairs up to the penthouse.

Alex and Trey entered the penthouse and Alex went to find Marian. He found her in the kitchen making a salad.

Alex went up behind her and put his arm around her, nuzzling her neck.

"Ummmm," said Mariam. "You had better watch out. My husband will be back soon."

"Tell him he's a lucky man," said Alex.

"I'm the lucky one," said Mariam turning and reaching for a kiss.

Alex kissed her and groaned.

"I have to go out. Trey is here and we have to go and pay a visit to Arnie Croan," said Alex.

"I thought you were going to wait until Lori and the baby were home before going to question Arnie," said Mariam.

"I was, but I had to call Trey in on another matter and he suggested we pay a short visit to Arnie so he can talk to his guardian angel and see if he can find out how bad the situation is before trying to fix it," said Alex.

Mariam nodded. "You two be careful. Lori and I don't want anything to happen to either of you," said Mariam.

"We will, I'm taking Micky along, and I won't be long," promised Alex.

He turned Mariam toward the front room, where Trey was waiting, with his arm still around Mariam they entered the room and Mariam greeted Trey with a smile.

"Hi, are Lori and Crystal still going home tomorrow?" asked Mariam.

Trey grinned and nodded. "Yes, we are all set for in the morning. Lori is anxious to get home and spend some time alone with just me and Crystal," said Trey. "We will have a few days before my dad and mom show up to meet their first grandchild."

Mariam shook her head and smiled. "Lori is afraid they will bring a cameraman with them," said Mariam.

Trey frowned. "If they do, I will lock the door and not let them in. My baby's homecoming is not going to be a media circus," he declared.

"We have to go. I won't be long," said Alex giving Mariam a quick kiss and heading for the door with Trey following.

Mariam watched them go and then turned toward the kitchen to finish making her salad.

Alex and Trey joined Micky in the basement garage, where he was waiting for them in front of the elevator. Alex took the front passenger seat and Trey climbed into the back.

Micky drove them straight to the Croan house. He had been to Sal and Sandy's parent's house many times, and he and Sal had followed two of Arnie's friends from the location the day they rescued Bobby,

He parked on the street in front of the house. The drive was full, with Arnie's car and his wife's car parked there. They all got out of the car and walked up the walk to the front door. Alex rang the doorbell.

Margo Croan opened the door and looked at them inquiringly.

"Hello, Mrs. Croan, I'm Alex Avorn. May I speak with your husband, please," said Alex.

"Who is it, Hun?" asked Arnie coming up behind his wife.

"It's Alex Avorn, He wants to speak with you," said Margo.

Arnie came around in front of Margo and looked at Alex and the others in surprise.

"Hello, Mr. Avorn," said Arnie. "What can I help you with?"

"Officer Croan, I'm Alex Avorn and these are my associates, Trey Loden and Micky Ansel. Your chief asked me to look into the death of Officer Kane. I would like to ask you a couple of questions about him, if you don't mind. I understand he was a friend of yours."

Arnie opened the door and motioned for them to enter. "Sure, come on in. I don't know how much help I'll be, but I'll be glad to help if I can."

Alex and the others entered the living room.

"Have a seat," said Arnie. "Would you like some coffee?"

"No, thank you. We won't be long. We just have a few questions," said Alex. Alex and Trey took chairs and Micky stood by the window. Trey didn't say anything. He was concentrating on trying to contact Arnie's guardian angel.

"Did you know Officer Kane was working undercover for the police department?" asked Alex.

"Yes, I did. I don't think he told anyone else, but he let it slip to me when he had too much to drink," said Arnie.

"Did you mention it to anyone else?" asked Alex.

"No, I wasn't sure if it was true or not. I didn't want to cause him any trouble, and I wasn't sure who I could trust," said Arnie. "Why is the chief having you investigate? He has investigators in the department."

"He said he didn't want to be accused of trying to cover up a crime. He wanted an impartial investigation," said Alex.

Arnie nodded. "I wish I could help, but I don't know much about it, just what I heard around the station," he said.

"Did Officer Kane say anything about the child trafficking?" asked Alex.

"No, he never mentioned anything about it," said Arnie.

Alex looked at Trey who nodded slightly. He stood and Trey and Mickey prepared to follow Alex's lead.

"Thank you for talking with us, Officer Croan. I may get in touch with you again later, with more questions, if you don't mind," said Alex standing and holding his hand out to shake.

"Sure," agreed Arnie. "I'll be glad to help any way I can."

Arnie shook his hand and followed by shaking Trey's and Micky's.

Alex smiled and nodded to Margo, who had been a silent observer at their meeting.

"Mrs. Croan," he said. Margo smiled and nodded back.

The three left and did not talk until they were away from the house.

"I managed to put the listening devise under my chair," said Trey.

"Good," said Alex. "Did you pick up anything from his guardian angel?"

"Arnie doesn't acknowledge him. He said Arnie doesn't listen to him at all, but Arnie was lying when he said he knew about officer Kane being undercover. He had never talked to him about being undercover. If officer Kane was undercover, Arnie was unaware of it. I don't know why he lied, but he did. It is going to be hard to reprogram him. We need to find out how involved he is in everything before we decide to do anything. He may need to go to jail, especially if he has been helping those kids be taken," said Trey.

Trey was much more aware of children since he had his own child, now. He couldn't imagine anyone wanting to let people get away with hurting children.

"Did his guardian angel say anything about Arnie taking bribes?" asked Alex.

"No, Arnie has a block up. I will have to get through the block before I can find out anything except what he is thinking about at the time," said Trey.

"We will have to figure out a way to get Arnie alone so we can work on him," said Alex.

Micky had not been talking. He had been concentrating on driving and listening to the other two talking.

"What do we tell Sal and Sandy?" asked Micky as he drove into their garage.

"I'll talk to them," said Alex.

"Okay," said Micky as he dropped Alex and Trey off in front of the elevator, before going to park the car.

"I'll be heading back to the hospital," said Trey as they were standing waiting on the elevator.

Alex smiled. Thanks, for coming to help," he said.

"Let me know when you get ready to take another crack at Arnie," said Trey.

"I will," promised Alex going into the elevator.

Trey turned to go to his car and return to the hospital. He was excited to get back. This was the first time he had been away from Lori and Crystal since the birth, and he couldn't wait to be back with them.

Alex took the elevator to the third floor and then on to the sixth floor. He wanted to talk to the guys and fill them in and check on Bobby.

Andrew opened the door for Alex. He had seen him coming.

Alex smiled at them as he entered. They were all gathered around, waiting to hear what he had to say.

"There is nothing conclusive, yet," said Alex. Arnie has a wall up blocking his guardian angel. Trey will have to get through the wall. We will do it at a later time. He claimed to know his friend was working undercover, but his guardian angel said he was lying."

Minnie nodded. "I knew it was a lie. Those guys were evil when they were talking at my house,' she said.

Sandy put an arm around her. "You're safe now," he said.

"How is Bobby doing?" asked Alex. "Has he woken up again?"

"No, he's still sleeping," said Sal.

"Trey planted the listening devise. I was thinking. If Sal and Andrew were to visit the Mase home, Sal could go in to visit with his mom and Andrew could stay in the car and listen to what is being said next door. If Sal parks in the garage, neither, Arnie or Mrs. Mase will ever know Andrew is there. You won't have to worry about nosy dog walkers," concluded Alex with a smile.

Sal was grinning. "I like that idea," he said. "I can pick up some more of Mom's chocolate cake."

Sandy shook his head. "Depend on Sal to think with his stomach," said Sandy with a grin.

"Tell your mom I would like a sample of her famous chocolate cake," said Alex with a grin.

"I'll tell her," promised Sal. "You are in for a real treat."

"Mom will love that," said Sandy.

"When do you want us to go?" asked Andrew.

"Tomorrow, After Minnie's mom goes to work and his friends are there. We want to hear the friends talking together," said Alex.

Alex turned to leave. "I'll see you later. I promised Mariam I wouldn't be long."

Andrew went back to the monitors after Alex left. Alex had only been gone a couple of minutes when Micky joined them.

"Did Alex give you the news?" he asked as he entered the room.

"Yes, he stopped by and told us about your meeting with Arnie," said Sandy.

"Arnie is one of the most, cold bloodied dudes, I have ever seen," said Micky. "Nothing fazed him. He showed no feelings about his friend being killed and the thought of children being taken didn't register with him. He was as cool as a cucumber. I was watching him. All he was worried about was making a good impression. When he shook hands, as we were leaving, his hands were dry, and he wasn't nervous at all. I don't think I have ever met anyone quite like him before." Micky shook his head and turned toward the kitchen.

The others watched him leave in astonishment. Usually Micky was the quiet one. They couldn't believe his reaction to Arnie.

"I told you he was bad," said Minnie.

Sandy drew her close to his side and kissed her on the forehead.

"We believed you. It's just unusual for Micky to have such a strong reaction."

"Yeah," agreed Sal. "He's usually one of the calmer agents to work with."

Sal shook his head, "I will be glad when this case is finished, and we don't have to deal with Arnie anymore."

The others nodded agreement especially Minnie.

TWELVE

MINNIE LOOKED at Sandy and smiled. She looked happy, but tired.

Sandy turned to Sal, who was still concerned about his friend, Micky.

"I am taking Minnie next door so she can rest for a while. If there is any change with Bobby, let us know," said Sandy.

"Okay," agreed Sal with a brief smile before he started for the kitchen to check on Micky.

Sandy took Minnie's hand and started for the door.

Minnie pulled him to a stop. He looked at her in surprise.

"Let me check on Bobby before we go," said Minnie.

Sandy nodded in understanding and released her hand so she could go into Bobby's room. He stood waiting by the door for her return.

Andrew looked at him and shook his head with a grin. Sandy didn't see the grin; all of his concentration was on Minnie.

Minnie entered Bobby's room quietly and walked to his bedside. She stood looking down at him until Lila joined her at the bedside.

"He's resting better," said Lila.

Minnie smiled at Lila. "Good. Sandy and I are going next door to rest. If there is any change, please let us know," said Minnie.

Lila smiled and patted her shoulder.

"I will," she promised.

With one last look, Minnie turned and left the room. She joined Sandy at the door and smilingly took his hand as he opened the door and led the way to their room.

When they entered the room, Minnie looked up at Sandy. "I'm going to take a shower before I lay down for a rest," she said.

Sandy kissed her gently on the forehead. "Okay, would you like me to order some food?" he asked.

"I'm not very hungry," said Minnie. "Maybe a sandwich or a salad would be alright."

"Alright, I'll see what is available," he said giving her a hug before releasing her.

Minnie went into her room to get some clothes before going into the bathroom and getting ready to take a shower. She sighed. The shower would help her. Maybe it could relieve some of the stress she was under. Since she knew Bobby was doing better, she was a little less stressed out, but she was still worried about her mom. She would be glad when this was all over. She hated not being honest with her mom, but she couldn't put her mom in danger. Her mom had no idea what Arnie was capable of.

In the front room, Sandy ordered salad and sandwiches for him and Minnie. He also included a pitcher of sweet iced tea.

He sat on the sofa to wait for Minnie and took up the TV remote and started looking through the channels. The news didn't look interesting, so he started looking through the movies being shown. He saw where an old movie, one of his favorite movies, was starting in a few minutes. Sandy left the TV on the movie station and went to gather glasses and plates and forks for the salads. He placed them on the counter and went back to the sofa to wait on Minnie.

The movie came on and then the food was delivered. The movie was on a commercial, so Sandy took the food and put it on the counter.

He went to Minnie's door and knocked gently. There was no answer, so Sandy opened the door and looked inside.

Minnie was curled up on her bed in her dressed in a tee shirt. He went over and pulled a blanket over her gently, so he wouldn't wake her.

Sandy left her door cracked so he could hear if Minnie woke up. He looked at the food and decided to wait and eat with Minnie. He took the food and the tea and placed them in the refrigerator. When he was done, he went back to his movie. Sandy lay back on the sofa and prepared to enjoy the movie. He was glad Minnie was getting some rest. He knew how hard this whole situation was on her. He wished there was something he could do to make things easier for her, but he didn't know what would help. He couldn't do the things Trey could do. He could only be there for her and protect her.

"That is what she needs right now," said his guardian angel.

"I wish I could do more," said Sandy.

"What you are doing is what she needs right now. You are helping her feel safe and loved. She loves you and you love her. Don't worry, this will all be over soon and you two can start the rest of your lives together," said his guardian angel.

Sandy sighed and turned his attention back to the movie. He was missing a lot of the movie. He couldn't concentrate on it with his mind on Minnie.

Sandy pulled one of the throw pillows under his head and lay back on the sofa to get more comfortable while he watched the movie. He was soon fast asleep while the movie played on. It provided soothing background noise for him, but, did not disturb his sleep or dreams.

In his dreams, Sandy was lying next to Minnie with her close in his arms. They were both enjoying a much, needed rest and a break from all of their worries.

"It's as it should be," said his guardian angel. He and Minnie's guardian angels watched in satisfaction as Minnie and Sandy rested in their dream arms. The two guardian angels were there to watch over them and make sure they were safe and undisturbed.

It was several hours later when Minnie stirred and stretched. She was surprised to find herself covered with a blanket. She smiled as she thought about it. Sandy must have covered her up, she thought. She eased out of bed and after a quick trip to the bathroom; she looked into the front room. She heard the television on. Minnie looked around for Sandy.

She spotted him on the sofa and started toward him. Minnie stopped in front of the sofa and realized that Sandy was fast asleep. She stood gazing at him, with love shining in her eyes, for a couple of minutes.

Minnie was hungry; she had missed her meal because she had fallen asleep. She decided to see what Sandy had ordered for them to eat.

Minnie headed for the kitchen and looked in the refrigerator. She found the sandwiches and salads. She pulled everything out and placed it on the counter.

Minnie made herself a salad and poured a glass of sweet tea. Minnie was happily eating her salad alternating with bites of the chicken salad sandwich, when Sandy awoke and realized he could hear Minnie in the kitchen.

Minnie smiled up at him when he came into the kitchen and found her sitting at the counter eating.

"I was hungry," said Minnie.

"I think I will join you," said Sandy.

He came around the counter and leaned over and kissed her.

"Umm, it tastes good," he said.

Sandy took his plate and helped his self to a sandwich, a salad, and a glass of tea, before sitting on a stool beside Minnie and starting to eat. They ate without talking until they were not so hungry.

"Has there been any more news?" asked Minnie.

"No," Sandy glanced at his phone and saw there had been no calls.

"Everyone will be sleeping, now," said Sandy.

"I guess it is pretty late," said Minnie. "After my nap, I'm not sleepy."

They finished eating and cleaned up after themselves. Minnie put their leftovers back in the refrigerator. They refilled their iced tea glasses and took them with them to the front room and set them on the table in front of the sofa.

Minnie waited until Sandy settled down on the sofa before sitting down close to him. Sandy put his arm around her and drew her closer to his side.

Sandy held the remote and started changing channels to find something they could watch.

Minnie was watching him scroll through the channels.

"Stop," said Minnie.

Sandy stopped and backed up a station. He looked at the movie and glanced down at Minnie.

"You want to watch 'The Princess Bride?'" he asked with a grin.

Minnie nodded. "It is one of my favorite movies," she said looking up at him pleadingly.

Sandy shrugged. "It's fine with me. I haven't seen it in a while, but I did like it," he said.

Minnie squeezed his arm and snuggled in close.

"Thanks," she said.

"Don't you know I would do anything for you?" he asked giving her a quick kiss. "Even watch 'The Princess Bride.'"

Minnie hit his arm. "You said you liked it," she said.

"I do, I was teasing," said Sandy.

Minnie settled back in his arms. She laid her head on his chest and watched as the movie started.

Sandy smiled down at the top of her head and kissed her gently. He was so thankful she was here with him and not at home where she would have to deal with Arnie and his cop friends. He hoped Alex and Trey would soon be able to neutralize the group and erase the danger around the neighborhood where they had all grown up.

Sandy sighed. Keeping his family in the dark about what was going on was the best protection he could give them. He was glad Sal and Andrew were going over there tomorrow. They would be able to check on the children in the neighborhood. He hoped Arnie and his friends were not so stupid as to prey on the children in their own neighborhood, but he couldn't be sure. They had not shown to be very smart so far.

Minnie looked up at him.

"Are you watching the movie?" she asked.

"Yes, I am watching," said Sandy.

He tightened his arms and tried to let his thoughts rest so he could watch the movie with Minnie.

Minnie laughed and Sandy paid more attention. They had both seen the movie before, but Minnie had seen it so many times, she knew it by heart. She knew what was going to happen before it happened.

Sandy watched Minnie more than the movie. He loved watching the expressions crossing her face. The more into the movie they got, the more she relaxed. It was great to see her relax and enjoy herself, for once. It reminded him of when they were kids. She had tagged along with him, Sal, and Bobby. They had all treated her gently. It was as if she was theirs and they had to take care of her. He was glad now, to know she had been included and not left out.

The movie went to commercial and Minnie looked up at Sandy. She saw the look of caring on his face, and she raised her face for a kiss.

Sandy kissed her and when she pulled back, she looked into his face again. "What were you thinking about?" she asked.

"I was thinking about when we were kids," said Sandy.

"What about it?" asked Minnie puzzled?

"I was just thinking how lucky I was to be around and watch you grow up," said Sandy.

Minnie grinned. "I was the lucky one. I had three big strong brothers to protect me," she said.

"Brother?" protested Sandy.

"That was then. This is now, and I don't see you as a brother anymore," assured Minnie.

"Good," said Sandy as he proceeded to kiss her senseless.

When he drew back, Minnie found herself lying across his lap held close in his arms, breathing heavily.

"Definitely not a brother," said Minnie with a smile as she raised her face for another kiss.

"The Princess Bride" played on, but Sandy and Minnie missed it. They were otherwise occupied.

While Sandy and Minnie were enjoying The Princess Bride and each other, in the next room, Bobby was waking up. He looked around and wondered where he was. He felt the heaviness in his hand and looked at the cast on his fingers.

Lila saw him looking around and hurried to his side.

Bobby looked up at her and tried to speak, but he couldn't seem to make any words come out.

Lila held the glass of water close so he could drink through the straw.

Bobby drank thirstily. Lila pulled the glass away when she thought he had enough. She did not want him to drink too much and get sick.

Bobby tried to talk again. "Where am I?" he asked in a scratchy voice.

"You are in Avorn Security Building," said Lila.

"What am I doing here?" he asked.

"Sal and Sandy Mase brought you here," said Lila.

"Have I been in an accident?" asked Bobby looking at his hand again.

"I don't know the details," said Lila. "All I know is you were hurt, and you have been unconscious for a few days. The doctor will be able to tell you more in the morning."

"Are Sal and Sandy here?" asked Bobby.

"Sal is, but Sandy is in his room getting some sleep," said Lila.

"Could you ask Sal to come and talk to me," asked Bobby.

"Sure," agreed Lila. "You just relax, and I will see if he is still awake."

After one last check of her patient, Lila went into the front room to see if Sal was still awake.

Andrew was on the sofa sleeping. Lila turned to the kitchen and entering found Sal and Micky sitting at the table talking quietly.

They looked up inquiringly when Lila entered.

Lila smiled at them.

"What's up?" asked Micky.

"Bobby is awake, and he wants to talk to Sal," said Lila. Sal rose and followed Lila into Bobby's room.

Bobby gave a grimace of a smile when he saw Sal. Sal smiled back at him and went to his bedside.

"Hi," said Sal. "It's good to see you awake finally."

"What happened to me?" asked Bobby.

Sal looked at him alertly. "You don't remember?" he asked.

"Was I in an accident? Why was I brought here instead of a hospital?" asked Bobby.

"When Minnie said she couldn't get in touch with you, Sandy and I and some of our friends went looking for you. When we found you, we brought you here and called the doctor. We didn't want to take you to the hospital until we knew what was going on," said Sal.

"What was going on? Why was Minnie panicked because she couldn't reach me?" asked Bobby.

"As far as I can tell, you were working on a story for your newspaper. It was about drugs and child trafficking. Minnie was upset because she couldn't get in touch with you for a week. You were unconscious when we found you, so I don't know all of the details, but you had been beaten and your fingers on your right hand were broken," said Sal.

"Are you sure, you don't remember any of this? You have been awake a couple of times," said Sal.

Bobby shook his head slightly. "I don't remember anything about waking up before now," he said.

Lila came back to the bedside. "The doctor will be here soon," she said.

Sal smiled at her and nodded. "Good," he said.

Bobby settled back and closed his eyes. He had a lot to think about. He opened his eyes and looked at Sal. Is Minnie alright?" he asked.

"Yes, Sandy is looking after her. She is staying in the apartment next to this one," said Sal.

Bobby relaxed then and closed his eyes again.

Sal sighed. He was not going to be the one to tell Bobby his little sister and one of his best friends were in love. He would leave the pleasure of that to his brother and Minnie.

He didn't know how Bobby would deal with the news and Sal didn't think Bobby could handle anything else right now.

THIRTEEN

THE DOCTOR ARRIVED a short time later. While he was in checking on Bobby, Sal called Sandy.

"Hi, Sal is anything wrong?" asked Sandy.

"No, I just wanted to let you know Bobby woke up again. The doctor is with him now. He doesn't seem to remember anything that has happened," said Sal.

"How can he not remember what has happened? He remembered when he woke up before," said Sandy.

Minnie leaned back in his arms and looked inquiringly at Sandy at his words. Sandy squeezed her shoulder in reassurance. "

"I don't know what is going on," said Sal. "I'll have to talk to the doctor when he comes out of Bobby's room."

"Okay, Minnie and I will be right over," said Sandy.

He hung up the phone and helped Minnie stand as he rose from the sofa.

"Is Bobby alright?" asked Minnie.

"I think so," said Sandy. "Dr. Parks is with him now, and he seems to be having a problem remembering."

Sandy guided her toward the door. "I knew you would want to be there to talk to the doctor, so we can find out what is going on," said Sandy.

Sal opened the door for them before they could knock. "I didn't mean to wake you up so early. I just wanted to keep you updated," said Sal.

Minnie smiled. "We were already awake. We were watching a movie," said Minnie.

Sal smiled back at her. "What movie were you watching?" asked Sal.

"'The Princess Bride,'" said Minnie.

Sal looked at Sandy a smile on his face. "You were watching 'The Princess Bride?'" he asked.

Minnie looked at Sal sternly. "It's a very good movie," she said.

Sal nodded, the smile fading from his face. "I know," he said.

Minnie turned away satisfied with his answer.

Sandy looked at Sal and smiled. Sal grinned back at him. Neither of them wanted to upset Minnie.

They all turned toward the doctor when he and Lila came out of Bobby's room.

Dr. Parks seemed surprised to see all of them waiting for him. "Bobby's fine," he said.

"What about his memory?" asked Minnie.

"It is nothing to worry about. He is still disoriented. He may be perfectly alright next time he wakes up. We will have to wait and see," said Dr. Parks.

Dr. Parks turned to Lila. "Call me if anything else happens," he said.

Lila nodded and Dr. Parks said goodbye to all of them and left.

Sandy turned to Sal. "Have you managed to get any sleep?" he asked.

Sal shook his head. "I woke up Andrew and sent him and Micky home to get some sleep. It was my turn to be on watch," said Sal.

"Minnie and I have had some sleep earlier," said Sandy. "Why don't you go next door and take a nap?"

Sandy took out his key card to give it to Sal. "We will call you if anything happens. You don't want Mom to think you are not getting enough sleep," said Sandy.

Sal took the key card. "Wake me up when Andrew shows up so we can go see what Arnie is up to," said Sal.

"We will," promised Sandy.

When Sal was gone and Lila had gone back to Bobby's room, Sandy turned to Minnie. "We can start a pot of coffee and make some pancakes, if you would like," said Sandy.

Minnie grinned. "I like very much," she agreed.

Sandy put an arm around Minnie as they went to the kitchen.

While Sandy started the coffee maker, Minnie found a large bowl and started gathering the makings for pancakes.

When Sandy finished with the coffee, He turned to watch Minnie starting the batter and getting ready to start cooking. "Do you need some help?" asked Sandy.

"You can get out some plates and cups. We also need butter and syrup and forks," said Minnie.

She quickly put the first pancakes on a plate and started a new batch. While they were cooking, she added butter and syrup to the ones on the plate. When she had the second plate filled, Minnie put the pan to the side while she prepared the second plate of pancakes. When they were ready, Minnie looked in the refrigerator and took out a can of whipped cream and squirted it on the top of the pancakes on both plates. She then took both plates and put them on the table.

Sandy had poured two cups of coffee and placed them on the table. He put the sugar and creamer on table close to Minnie.

Sandy held Minnie's chair for her to sit down and then took the seat across from her. He then looked at the two plates and shook his head.

"They look almost too good to eat," he said.

"They taste even better," said Minnie taking a bite and savoring it.

Sandy carried his first bite to his mouth and, after chewing and swallowing; he quickly took a second bite.

Minnie grinned as she watched him enjoying the pancakes. She was also continuing to enjoy her own plate.

Lila came into the kitchen as they were finishing eating.

"I thought I smelled pancakes," said Lila.

"I have some more batter made. I can cook you some," said Minnie.

"I would love some," said Lila getting out a plate and pouring herself a cup of coffee.

When Minnie put her pancakes on the plate and squirted whipped cream on them, Lila smiled and thanked her before taking her plate and going to the table.

"Would you like some more?" Minnie asked Sandy.

"Yes, please," said Sandy with a smile. "These were great."

"They taste wonderful," agreed Lila. "I don't think I have ever seen anyone put whipped cream on pancakes outside of a pancake house."

"It sure makes them special," said Sandy. "I'm going to make sure we keep a can of whipped cream in the refrigerator from now on."

Minnie smiled. She was happy her pancakes had been liked. She started cleaning the kitchen and loading the dishwasher.

Lila finished eating and after thanking her for the pancakes, she started back to Bobby's room.

"We can watch Bobby if you want to catch a nap," said Sandy.

Lila looked over at them. "You wouldn't mind?" she asked.

"We wouldn't mind at all," said Minnie. "We have already had some sleep and are wide awake."

"I'll just check to see if he is okay and then I will lie down for a while, thanks," said Lila.

Sandy and Minnie passed Lila as she was on her way to her room to sleep. They were headed for the front room.

"He's fine. I left the door open so you can hear him if he stirs," said Lila. "If he wakes, come and get me."

"We will, don't worry. Have a nice nap," said Minnie.

Lila smiled and went to her room. Minnie and Sandy looked in on Bobby and satisfied he was sleeping, they continued on into the living room. They sat on the sofa, close together with Sandy's arm holding her close. They did not want to turn on the television because, they were afraid they might not hear Bobby over the sound.

They sat there softly talking and making plans for their future.

Andrew, Sal, and Micky all arrived at the door at the same time the next morning.

Sandy opened the door and smiled at the group.

"Good, you are all here. Minnie has pancakes made for you, so go and eat while they are hot," he said.

They all headed for the kitchen. When they saw the plates of pancakes, with whipped cream, on the table, they hurriedly took their seats.

Sandy passed around cups of coffee. The guys ate quickly with enjoyment. When they finished, they thanked Minnie for the pancakes, and all headed for the living room to talk about the day's assignment.

Minnie shook her head and started filling the dishwasher.

"Are you guys all set to listen in on Arnie?" Sandy asked Sal and Andrew.

"We are all set, but Andrew is going to be doing the listening. I'm going to be talking Mom out of some chocolate cake," said Sal.

Sandy shook his head. "You are spoiled," he said.

Sal nodded his head and smirked at Sandy. "Mom loves to spoil me," he said. "It makes her happy and my stomach is happy also."

"Be sure you don't say anything to make Mom suspicious. She is a very smart lady," said Sandy.

"I know," agreed Sal. "I never could get anything past her. I plan on saying as little as possible and just being my charming self."

Sandy shook his head. "Sal's guardian angel will keep a watch on him. Don't worry," reassured his guardian angel.

"Good, that makes me feel better," thought Sandy.

Sal and Andrew looked at the time and decided to start for Sal and Sandy's home.

Micky looked around as if he felt a little lost without Sal, who was his usual partner.

"They will be fine," reassured Sandy. "Alex is sending Sal because he can visit without blowing our cover."

"I know," said Micky. "I was wondering what Alex has for me to do today."

"I think he wants us to be on standby. If we can find out where they are holding their victims, we may be able to rescue them," said Sandy.

"That would be wonderful," said Minnie overhearing their conversation as she entered the room.

"Has Lila awakened, yet?" he asked.

"I heard her stirring. She will be out soon," said Minnie heading for Bobby's room to check on him.

Minnie stood at Bobby's bedside looking down at him. She was wondering if she would ever have her big brother back like he was before all of this happened.

She sighed and wiped away the tears from her misty eyes. Crying and feeling sorry for herself would not help anything. She would have to deal with what she had to face.

"It will be alright. It may not be the same as before, but you are not the same as before. Life changes everyone and you move forward and deal with it. You all will be fine with our help," said her guardian angel.

"I know you are right, and I love that you are with me to help and protect me. I will be brave and listen to your advice," thought Minnie.

Lila joined her at Bobby's bedside.

"Did you manage to sleep?" asked Minnie.

"Yes, thank you for watching Bobby for me. I had a lovely sleep," said Lila with a smile, as she started checking Bobby to see if there had been any change.

Minnie watched her closely, she could not tell what Lila was thinking.

"Is he alright," asked Minnie when Lila turned away to write her findings down for the doctor report.

"He is doing fine. He should be waking up again, soon. He is not as deep asleep as he was," said Lila.

Minnie gave a happy grin to Lila and went to join Sandy and Micky in the front room.

Sal and Andrew arrived at the street where the Croan and the Mase houses were located. As Sal drove by the Croan house Margo Croan was backing her car out of her drive to go to work.

She waved at Sal and he waved back.

Andrew had scrunched down so she had less chance of seeing him. Sal drove up into the garage at the Mase house.

"If you need me, call me on my cell phone," said Sal.

Andrew nodded and started getting set up to listen in next door.

Sal turned and went inside through the garage door. It led into the kitchen. His mom was cleaning the kitchen and loading the dishwasher. She turned and smiled at Sal with a pleased look on her face.

"Well, you did manage another visit," she said happily.

Sal went over and gave her a hug.

"You know I'll stop by anytime I can," said Sal.

"How did you know I had another chocolate cake made?" asked his Mom.

"I came to see you," said Sal. "You know I will never turn down your chocolate cake. Even our boss wanted me to see if you would make him and Mariam a sample."

"You let your boss sample my cake?" asked his Mom.

"No, there wasn't any left when he came by. He heard all of us talking about how good it was and decided he would like to try it for himself. I told him I would ask you," said Sal.

Mrs. Mase shook her head, but she was pleased. "I'll make one for him and his wife and you can come by and get it and take it to him," she said.

Sal kissed her cheek. "Thanks, Mom," he said.

"Are you going to be able to stay for a while?" she asked.

"I can stay for a bit," said Sal. "I'm waiting for a call about a case we are on."

"Would you like some breakfast or coffee?" she asked.

"I've had breakfast, but I would love some coffee," said Sal'

"Sit at the table. I'll get it for you," instructed his Mom.

She poured him a cup of coffee and placed it in front of him. After getting her own cup, she sat at the table across from him.

"How's Sandy doing?" she asked.

"He's fine. He was busy working on another case this morning. I'm sure you will be hearing from him soon," said Sal grinning to himself.

His Mom looked at him curiously, but she didn't ask what he meant.

"How is Dad doing?" asked Sal. "He's not working too hard and overdoing it, is he?"

"He's fine. I keep a close watch on him, and his guardian angel will let me know if there is cause for concern," said Mrs. Mase.

Sal grinned.

"Why are you smiling?" she asked.

"I was just thinking how happy I am. You guys have never made any difficulties about us speaking with our guardian angels. It was so good to know we could talk to you about them and you would believe us," said Sal.

His Mom patted his hand on the table. "As long as you did not talk to other people and draw attention to yourselves and us, we were happy to know you accepted them and believed in them," she said. "They made it a lot easier for us when you were growing up. We knew you were being looked after. It took a big load off my mind, especially when you started dating,"

Sal flushed slightly. "They didn't talk to you guys about us dating, did they?" he asked.

His Mom patted his hand again and smiled widely. "Of course not," she said. "They just let us know not to worry."

Sal shook his head. "I am going to have a talk with a certain guardian angel," he said. "Just wait until I tell Sandy." His guardian angel was being very quiet.

Mrs. Mase burst out laughing. "Don't pick on them. I am sure they kept all of your secrets," she said.

Sal's phone rang and he quickly answered it,

"They are headed to one of the houses where they keep kids," said Andrew. "Call Alex, I'll be right there," said Sal.

"I have to go," said Sal getting up and hugging his Mom.

"Do you want to take some cake with you?" she asked. "I'll have to get it later," said Sal as he hurried out the door. He hurried to his car and quickly drove from the garage.

"Do you know where they are headed?" asked Sal.

"They didn't give the address. They only said the kids at Kennis house were being moved out," said Andrew. "Alex is sending Sandy and Micky to help. He said for us to try and follow without being spotted and he will have them intersect with us so we can turn like we are not following. He said for us to listen to our guardian angels, and call when we get close, he is going to have the FBI on standby. He said he is going to call the chief, but he is going to tell him to keep it quiet until he knows who can be trusted."

"I see the car we trailed the other day. It's up ahead of us about five cars," said Andrew. "There is Mickey and Sandy. We can go up another block and turn and make a block to come at them from a different angel."

"My guardian angel said to call in the troops. He said we are close to Kennis house. He got the information from their guardian angels," said Sal. "He said the address is 1147."

"Alex, the address is 1147 Kennis," said Andrew. "He's sending help."

They followed the guardian angel directions to the house and saw some men herding some children toward a couple of vans parked in front of the house.

Sal stopped his car and saw Micky stop, also. The guys were not paying any attention to them. Their attention was on getting the children loaded in the vans. Sal and Micky, followed by Sandy and Andrew, started running toward the men. Sal and Micky dropped kicked the two guys and proceeded to knock them out. Sandy and Andrew started drawing the children away where they would not get hurt. Sal saw the car they had been following slow down and then keep going when they saw what was happening.

FOURTEEN

THE FBI SQUEALED to a stop in front of the house. They took over taking the men into custody and taking the children to the hospital to be checked out.

Sal called Alex and filled him in. He asked what they should do. Alex told them to come on in and let the FBI handle it. The guys started for home and Alex called the chief and filled him in.

Sal had to make one stop on the way home. This time, he took Andrew in to meet his Mom while he picked up his chocolate cake. His mom even had a cake ready to be taken to Alex and Mariam.

"Mom, you are the best," said Sal giving her a hug and kissing her cheek.

Andrew nodded and agreed around a mouthful of chocolate cake. "Thank you, Mrs. Mase, this is the best chocolate cake I have ever tasted." Mrs. Mase flushed with happiness.

After finishing the cake, Sal and Andrew left for Avorn Security Building. They carried a cake for Alex and Marian, and some slices of cake for themselves and the rest of their group.

When they entered the building, Sal called Alex and asked him to meet him on the sixth floor. He told him to bring Mariam if he could.

"My mom wanted me to give you a gift," said Sal.

"Alright," agreed Alex. "Mariam and I will be down as soon as she gets back from downstairs. Today was one of her days to read stories to the children in day care."

Sandy and Micky were already there when Sal and Andrew entered the apartment. Sandy grinned when he smelled the chocolate cake and saw Sal and Andrew each carrying a large container.

Sal shook his head when he saw Sandy smiling.

"One is for Alex and Mariam. They will be here to pick it up soon," said Sal.

"From the size of the container, I would say there is plenty for all of us," said Sandy.

Sal carried his container of cake and placed it on the counter in the kitchen and went to get paper plates and forks. Andrew placed the cake for Alex and Mariam on the table.

Everyone gathered around to be sure and receive a slice. Minnie took a plate and carried it to Lila. When she returned, Sandy had a plate saved for her, and was busy eating his own. Sal, Micky and Andrew were all busy enjoying their slices.

They were just finishing when Alex and Mariam arrived. When Sal presented them with the cake from his mom, there were big smiles on both of their faces.

"Tell your Mom thanks. It smells delicious," said Mariam. "We can take a couple of slices to Lori and Trey when we take them some food tonight. The cake will top off the meal nicely."

"What happened after we stopped those child traffickers?" asked Micky.

"I talked to the Chief at the police department," said Alex. "He wants us to stay on the case. He still wants to find out why his officer was shot. He would like to clear the police department of any involvement, if he can. The two men are in the custody of the FBI. The children are being checked out at the hospital and Child Protective

Services are locating their parents and reuniting them with their children. I will keep up with what is being done and be sure all of the children have a home to return to."

"Have you decided what we are going to do about Arnie?" asked Sandy.

"I am going to see how soon Trey can work with him and have him come down to Avorn Security for more questions. We are either going to change his attitude or have him put away for the crimes he has committed," said Alex.

"I hope something can be done, soon," said Minnie. "I hate to have to keep lying to my mom about where I am."

"It should be tomorrow or the next day," said Alex.

Minnie smiled at him in thanks and snuggled close to Sandy. He tightened his arm around her and held her protectively.

"Thank Mrs. Mase for the cake for us," said Alex. "Mariam and I have to go. We have food waiting downstairs to take to Lori and Trey."

"We didn't want Lori to have to cook on her first day from the hospital," said Mariam. "Besides, I get to hold my beautiful goddaughter."

Everyone smiled and sent best wishes to Trey and Lori.

When Alex and Mariam were gone, they all went into the living room to check out the news on the television. They wanted to see what was being reported about the arrest by the FBI.

The news was on and they were not surprised to hear the FBI taking credit for the bust and the rescue of the children. The guys just shook their heads and didn't say anything.

They didn't want the publicity anyway. Having the spotlight on them would make it harder for them to do some of the jobs they did. They always tried to stay out of the spotlight when they could.

Shortly after listening to the news, Micky and Sal said goodnight and left. Sandy and Minnie checked on Bobby before leaving for their room. Andrew was staying there to keep a watch on Bobby and Lila.

It had been a long day for Sandy and Minnie so, after taking a shower, they both decided to take a nap. Minnie went first and was already asleep when Sandy emerged from the bathroom. He stood looking down at her as she slept. He pulled a blanket over her, gently to keep from waking her.

"She looks so beautiful," whispered Sandy. "Yes, she does," agreed his guardian angel. "I am the luckiest man in the world," said Sandy. "When anyone finds their true love and their love is returned, the guardian angels rejoice. They know their help has made the world a better place for people in love," said his guardian angel.

Sandy sighed and went to his room to get some sleep. He left the door to both rooms open so he would hear if there was any trouble.

When Sal and Micky were on their way out of the building, they met Sally Swills as she was leaving the beauty parlor. She was getting ready to pick up her nephew from daycare, but she stopped when Sal and Micky came into view.

With a big smile on her face, she turned to talk to them. "I don't know what Mr. Avorn did, but I received a call from the judge, she wants to meet with me and Andy tomorrow about the custody case. Please, tell Mr. Avorn I appreciate his help. No matter how it turns out, thank him for trying," she said.

"We will tell him," agreed Micky with a smile. "I hope it all works out for all of you."

"At least, the judge is finally listening. It's more than we were able to accomplish before," said Sally. "I have to pick up my nephew. Thank you for helping us." Sally turned and headed for the daycare.

The guys watched her until she disappeared into the daycare room before turning and heading for the elevator to the garage and their cars. They waved goodbye as the cars came into view. Each went to their car and left, headed for home and a good night's sleep.

Andrew was channel surfing. It was one of his favorite past times. He loved keeping an eye on the building security. He was very interested in how well the guards functioned on their patrols through the building. Alex knew about Andrew's habit of keeping an eye on the building. He didn't say anything to him about it. He decided a little extra attention in the building was good for them all.

Lila came out of Bobby's room. She was on her way to the kitchen, but she stopped and watched the screens as Andrew scanned the building. Andrew looked over at her and grinned.

"Do all of the hallways have cameras?" asked Lila.

"Yes, also the elevators and the garage." said Andrew. "Alex thought it would be a bad advertisement for our firm if we couldn't protect ourselves and our tenants from harm. Besides, he is determined to keep witch hunters away from Mariam and anyone else they may go after when they find out about our guardian angels. We have a security office on the third floor. They keep watch on the building twenty-four hours a day."

Lila nodded. "I can understand. My parents made sure our family didn't talk about our guardian angels," she said. "It is only recently things have relaxed enough we can talk about them. People are becoming much more accepting of their guardian angels."

"Our guardian angels have been a big help to us," said Andrew. "They have warned us of danger and helped to communicate with other guardian angels to find missing people and to find out what is true in other situations. They also help us to recognize our true loves. Do you need any help? Is Bobby alright?" he asked.

"Bobby is sleeping. I thought I would make me a sandwich and get a drink before he wakes," said Lila. Andrew rose and started for the kitchen with her. Lila smiled at him. "You don't have to come with me. I can manage."

"I think I'll make me a sandwich, too," said Andrew. "As good as Mrs. Maze's cake is, I need some solid food." They worked together to make the sandwiches and took them, along with two glasses of tea, into the front room and sat on the sofa. They used the coffee table to hold their food. Andrew turned the television on, and they watched the evening news while they ate.

There was a recap of the earlier story. It was the same as before. The FBI was sticking with their story. This time the Chief made an appearance and thanked the FBI for their help in recovering the children and bringing their captors to justice.

Andrew laughed. "I bet the Chief had to grit his teeth to get that statement out," he said.

Lila laughed. "It's all about keeping the public happy so they will keep him in office. He doesn't want anyone to think he is not doing his best to keep the city safe."

"To be fair," said Andrew. "He is doing the best he can. He did call on Avorn Security for help. He could have tried to cover for his officers. Instead, he is trying to find the truth."

"You are right," agreed Lila. "I hadn't thought about it like that. He is willing to risk looking bad to find the truth. That takes a strong determination to do what is right."

There was a noise from Bobby's room and Lila rose to go check on him. She started to take her plate and glass to the kitchen, but Andrew stopped her. He rose and removed the plate from her hand and placed it with his.

"You go ahead and check on Bobby. I will take these into the kitchen with mine," he said.

"Thanks," said Lila. She gave Andrew her glass and hurried into Bobby's room.

Bobby was awake and looking around. He looked at Lila, sharply, when she entered his room. He relaxed when he saw it was her.

Lila smiled at him and went to the side of the bed to check on him.

"You decided to join us again," remarked Lila.

Bobby grimaced and winced in pain. Lila was watching him closely. She saw the evidence of pain on his face.

"The doctor left some pain medicine for you to have when you awakened," she said. Lila went to get the medicine to add to his IV bag. "This is a light dose. We don't want to make you go back to sleep. It will do you good to stay awake for a while," she said. "Do you remember what happened to you?" she asked.

Bobby thought for a minute. "Yeah, I met with an informant. He gave me some more information for my story. I had met with him before so I wasn't as vigilant as I should have been. As soon as he left, two of Arnie's friends jumped me. They had another guy with them. They took the information I had just received and tied me to a chair. They tried to find out how much information I had already collected. I didn't tell them anything, so they kept beating me. I didn't think I was going to make it out of there alive," said Bobby.

"You almost didn't," said Lila.

"I need to let Mr. Avorn know you are awake. It's thanks to him and your friends you are alive," said Lila.

Bobby relaxed as the pain medication started to ease his pain. "I seem to remember my sister being here along with Sal and Sandy Mase," he said.

"Yes," agreed Lila. "Minnie is next door. Sandy is watching over her. I'll let them know you are awake."

"No," said Bobby. "Let her sleep. I will talk to them later. I want to wait until things are clearer in my mind. I am still a little fuzzy about things right now. Waking them up is not going to help me think."

Lila stopped and thought about his words and finally nodded. "Okay, I'll wait, after all you are a lot better now than you were the last time you were awake," she said. "Maybe a little thinking time will be good for you. Andrew is in the front room. I have to let him know you are awake. He may want to talk to you."

"Okay," agreed Bobby.

Lila went to the front room to let Andrew know Bobby was awake and aware of his situation.

Andrew followed Lila to Bobby's room to talk with him. He came to the bedside and grinned at Bobby. "I'm glad you are back with us," said Andrew.

"So am I," agreed Bobby. "I owe you guys my life. They had just about decided I was not going to tell them anything and they were getting ready to finish me off."

Andrew smiled. "We had to get you out of there. Minnie would have never let us forget it if we hadn't saved you," he replied.

Bobby tried to smile, but it was more of a grimace. "I left some papers with Minnie. I didn't mean to put her in danger," said Bobby.

"Minnie turned the papers you left over to Alex and He sent copies to the FBI and the police chief. One of the guys, holding you prisoner was killed and the chief hired Avorn Security to investigate and find out who killed him. We have been watching Arnie and his friends. Tonight, we stopped one of the child traffickers and freed some children. We sent two of the men to jail. The FBI is taking credit for the bust. I think Alex called them so the spotlight would not be on us. He wants us to keep a low profile," said Andrew.

I'm glad some of the children will be going home," said Bobby. "Do you have anything on Arnie?"

"Nothing concrete, we have suspicions, but most of the evidence points to his friends," said Andrew.

"I was having the same problem. I found plenty of evidence against his friends, but it was harder to pin Arnie down," said Bobby.

"Alex is going to let Trey talk to Arnie's guardian angel so we can see if Arnie can be helped," said Andrew.

"I hope it works," said Bobby around a large yawn.

"I think I need to let you get some more rest," said Andrew. "I don't want to tire you out and cause a relapse. You get some sleep and maybe you will be ready for everyone's questions in the morning."

"Okay," agreed Bobby. He was falling asleep as Andrew left the room. Lila checked him and made sure he was covered and sleeping before she followed Andrew into the front room.

"Is he going to be alright?" asked Andrew.

"He's going to be fine. He was clear and alert when he awakened this time. I'll have to check with the doctor to be sure, but I think he is on his way to recovery," said Lila. "Since he is sleeping, I think I will turn in myself. If he wakes up, will you come and wake me?" asked Lila.

"Sure, I'll be glad to. Have a good night. If you need anything, let me know," said Andrew.

"I'm fine, good night," said Lila as she turned and went to her room.

Andrew watched her go. He shook his head. There goes a fine-looking woman, he thought. "She is too old for you," said his guardian angel. "She is not for you. Be patient, your own true love will be showing up before too much longer. You don't need to complicate things by chasing the wrong woman,"

Andrew grinned. "So, I have a true love to wait for," he said.

"Of course, you do," replied his guardian angel. "If you pay attention, I will help you to know when she arrives."

Andrew lay back on the sofa and left the television running. He wasn't watching the show. He was thinking about having his own true love. He was very excited at the prospect of a love of his own. He sighed loudly. He was so ready to make a life with someone special.

FIFTEEN

ALEX ALONG WITH SAL, Sandy, and Minnie gathered in Bobby's room the next morning. Minnie stayed back with Lila and let the men talk to Bobby. After he explained about his dealings with the informant and his capture and torture, Alex decided it was time to arrange for Arnie to be questioned by Trey. They needed to know just how involved he was in taking payoffs to hide the breaking of the law.

Alex called Arnie and arranged for him to come to Avorn Security later that morning. He then called Trey and asked him to be there for the questioning and reprogramming. Trey asked for several of the men to be there as well. He wanted to use all of their guardian angel power to help Arnie's guardian angel get control of Arnie. Lori had loaned Mariam her special ring to help put Arnie to sleep, so Mariam was going to be at the meeting as well.

Mariam was a little nervous about using Lori's ring. Lori had explained how to use it the night before when Alex and Mariam were visiting.

When Arnie arrived at Avorn Security Building, he was instructed by the guard at the front desk to take the elevator to the third floor. When he reached the third floor, Brenda was waiting to show him into the conference room. Inside the conference room, Micky, Sal, Sandy, and Trey were already waiting along with Alex and Mariam.

Arnie looked around in Surprise to see so many people waiting for him. Ales came forward to greet him. "Hello, Officer Croan, I'm Alex Avorn. Thank you for coming down." Alex held out his hand to shake Arnie's hand. Arnie extended his hand for a handshake.

"It was no problem. I'm glad to help any way I can," said Arnie.

Alex drew Mariam forward. "This is my wife, Mariam." Arnie extended his hand to shake the hand Mariam was holding out to him. When they shook hands, Arnie felt a small prick as the ring injected him with the sleeping drought.

"It's nice to meet you," said Mariam. "I'll leave you to your business. I have an appointment." Mariam gave Alex a quick kiss and left the room.

Alex smiled as Mariam left the room. "Have a seat Officer Croan. This won't take long. There are just a few details we need to clarify." Alex waited until Arnie seated himself and took his own seat. "You have met Trey and Micky and I'm sure you know Sal and Sandy Mase." Arnie nodded to each one as Alex drew his attention to them. They all nodded back.

Arnie was beginning to get woozy. He shook his head to clear it. He looked at Alex suspiciously. "Did you drug me?" he asked.

Alex looked at him in surprise. "How could I have drugged you, Officer?" he asked. When it looked like Arnie was about to fall out of his chair, Alex motioned for the guys to catch him and tie him to the chair. Arnie was so out of it he was not aware of being tied.

Alex sat back and let Trey take over. Trey closed his eyes and concentrated on drawing all of the guardian angels in the room forward to help.

"Help me tear down the wall," he said softly. "One brick at a time, help to clear a pathway for Arnie's guardian angel to follow. That is the way. Help Arnie to understand. He needs to switch to the day shift. He can no longer be around in the day to hang out with his friends. He will spend his time off work with the wife he loves. He will support his stepdaughter's choice of a groom. He will be friendly to his stepson. He will stay away from anything illegal He will not remember this message, but he will follow it and change his life accordingly. Tell him to break off with his friends slowly so they will not hold a grudge against him or his family. He will not remember anything about what the officer, who was killed, was doing. He will only remember the officer telling him about working undercover trying to get evidence against the drug dealers.

When he wakes up, Arnie will not remember any of this. He will feel good and refreshed. He had a nice talk with Mr. Avorn and answered all his questions. There is nothing to worry about"

Trey opened his eyes and nodded for the guys to untie Arnie, who was beginning to stir awake. They untied him and took their seats to wait and see what Arnie would do.

Arnie shook his head and looked around.

"Thank you for coming in and answering my questions, Officer. I appreciate your help," said Alex rising and holding out his hand to Arnie.

"Sure," said Arnie shaking Alex's hand "I'm glad I could help. If you need any more information, I'll be glad to do what I can, but I have to leave for the station. I'm putting in for a daytime shift so I can spend more time with my wife."

"Good luck, I hope everything works out for you," said Alex walking Arnie to the door and watching until he was in the elevator leaving.

Alex turned back to Trey. "What did you find out?"

"Arnie was not taking payoffs, but he knew his friends were. They were trying to get him involved. He was resisting, but they were wearing him down. The officer, who was shot, really was working undercover. The drug dealers found out. That is why they shot him. He had let it slip to Arnie and his friends when he was drunk. Arnie thinks one of the others rated him out, but he doesn't know for sure. I think Arnie will be alright if he can stay away from the others. At least he has a chance, now," stated Trey with a shrug. "His guardian angel will be able to influence him, now."

"We will just have to wait and see," agreed Alex. "I will let the Chief know what we have learned and see if he wants us to keep digging." He turned to the others. "Sal, Micky, Brenda has a missing person case for you to start working on. If you will check with her as you leave you can get started on it."

"Yes, Sir," said Sal and Micky. They rose from their seats and started for the door. Sandy started to follow, but Alex stopped him with an upraised hand.

"Sandy, I hope you don't think I am interfering, but I have noticed how close you and Minnie are becoming. Are you planning to get married?" asked Alex.

"Yes, Sir," said Sandy with a smile.

"I understand Minnie is starting college to be a teacher," said Alex. Sandy nodded. He was puzzled as to why Alex was asking about Minnie's plans. "When you are married, Minnie will be part of the Avorn family. Avorn furnishes a scholarship to college for relatives of our employees. Minnie will be eligible for it. Ask her to apply as soon as possible."

Sandy had a big grin on his face. "Yes, Sir, thank you. I'll tell her," said Sandy. He hurried from the room to go and give Minnie the news.

When Sandy arrived at Bobby's room, he found Minnie sitting at his bedside talking to him quietly. Sandy hurried in. He looked so, happy, Minnie looked at him curiously. Sandy filled Bobby in on what had happened with Arnie. Both Minnie and Bobby drew a sigh of relief. They were happy ofor their mom. They had been worried about how she would react if Arnie had to go to jail. It was a relief to know she would be alright. When he finished telling Bobby about the meeting, Sandy drew Minnie up into his arms.

"Your sister and I are going to be married, Bobby, just as soon as you can walk her down the isle. I love her very much and she loves me," said Sandy kissing her lightly while Bobby watched from his bed with a smile.

"I know," said Bobby. "Minnie told me."

Sandy looked down into Minnie's eyes and smiled. "I talked to Sal. He said that since our apartment is a two bedroom, it would be better for Micky to move in with him. We can move into Micky's apartment. It's a one bedroom and we would have more privacy. Minnie smiled and hugged Sandy. Alex told me to tell you to apply for the Avorn scholarship to pay for college. It is available to all his employees and their families. You will be eligible for it as soon as we are married. He said not to wait to apply."

Minnie looked at Sandy as if she couldn't believe what she was hearing, then, she squealed and started jumping up and down while Sandy and Bobby watched indulgently. She stopped and flung her arms around Sandy and kissed him.

"Thank you," she thought to her guardian angel.

"It's always a pleasure to help find true love," replied a very satisfied guardian angel.

The End

Dear reader,

We hope you enjoyed reading *Love's Helper*. Please take a moment to leave a review, even if it's a short one. Your opinion is important to us.

Discover more books by Betty McLain at https://www.nextchapter. pub/authors/betty-mclain

Want to know when one of our books is free or discounted? Join the newsletter at http://eepurl.com/bqqB3H

Best regards,

Betty McLain and the Next Chapter Team

The story continues in:
Love's Tuna Salad by Betty McLain

To read the first chapter for free, please head to:
https://www.nextchapter.pub/books/loves-tuna-salad

ABOUT THE AUTHOR

With five children, ten grandchildren and six great-grandchildren, I have an extremely busy life, but reading and writing have always been a large and enjoyable part of my life. I've been writing since I was young. I wrote stories in notebooks and kept them private. They were all handwritten, because I was unable to type. We lived in the country, and I had to do most of my writing at night. My days were busy helping with my brothers and sister. I also helped Mom with the garden and canning food for our family. Even though I was tired, I still managed to get my thoughts down on paper at night.

When I married and began raising my family, I continued writing my stories while helping my children through school and then transitioning into their own lives and families. My sister was the only one to read my stories. She was very encouraging. When my youngest daughter started college, I decided to go to college myself. I had already completed my GED and only had to take a class to prepare for my college entrance tests. I passed with flying colors and even managed to get a partial scholarship. I took computer classes to learn typing. The English and literature classes helped me polish my stories.

I found that public speaking was not for me. I was much more comfortable with the written word, but researching and writing the speeches was helpful. I was able to use those skills to build a story.

I finished college with an associate degree and a 3.4 GPA. I earned several awards, including the President's List, Dean's List, and Faculty List. My school experience helped me gain more confidence with writing. I want to thank my college English professor for boosting my confidence with writing by telling me that I had a good imagination. She said I told an interesting story. My daughter, who is an excellent writer and has published many books, convinced me to publish some of my stories. She used her experience self-publishing to publish my stories for me. The first time I held one of my books and looked at my name on it as the author, I was proud. It was well received. Which encouraged me to continue writing and publishing. I have been building my library of books since then. I've also written and illustrated several children's books.

Being able to type my stories opened up a whole new world for me. Access to a computer helped me research anything I needed to know and expanded my ability to keep writing my books. Joining Facebook and making friends all over the world expanded my outlook considerably. I was able to understand many different lifestyles and incorporate them into my stories.

Ever heard the saying, watch out what you say, and don't make the writer mad. You may end up in a book being eliminated." Well, it is true. All of life is there to stimulate your imagination. It is fun to develop a story and to watch it come alive in your mind. When I get started, the stories almost write themselves; I just have to get all of it down as the ideas come to me, before they're gone.

I love knowing that the stories I have written are being read and enjoyed by others. It is awe-inspiring to look at the books and think, "I wrote that."

I look forward to many more years of creating and distributing my stories, and I hope the people reading my books are looking forward to reading them just as much as I enjoy writing them.

BOOKS BY BETTY MCLAIN

~

Rich Man's daughter

Dody

~

Love's Magic Series

Love's Magic

Love's Dream

Love's Time

Love's Reflection

Love's Call

Love's Prophesy

Love's Sight

Love's Answer

Love's Enemy

Love's Retaliation

Love's Obsession

Love's Memory

Love's Gamble

Love's Plea

Love's Promise

Love's Voice

Love's Helper

Lightning Source UK Ltd.
Milton Keynes UK
UKHW010954280820
368951UK00004B/137